CHILDREN OF UMA

A Post Apocalyptic Adventure for

By Geo Collazo & John McGuire

"Speed is a byproduct. Going fast. But remember: the car is you, you are the car."

- Memphis Raines

Table Of Contents

Foreword by Geo

I was driving my car down River Road when I stopped to let a clan of geese cross. A month into the pandemic and nature had excitedly reclaimed the world. Geese luxuriated in non-existent traffic. The sky was brighter.

The end of days.

It was a shared experience across the globe.

That summer, John started working on 3,2,1...Action! That winter, I came along to help. We launched our first two Action books while I was percolating a story about how everything old is new again.

A far-away war. A plague. The dust bowl. The Great Depression. Who gets forgotten? What kind of life do they live?

I blended those questions with the Mad Max series and looked for touching moments in that film, such as the relationship between Wez and the Golden Youth, which I interpreted as a love story when I was younger.

My answer was an RPG that approached the apocalypse from a different angle, in a different location than usual, and with some human stories open to various interpretations.

Something complex but with simple, intuitive rules.

Anyway, I hope I accomplished a bit of that.

Also, I still break for geese.

Content Warnings, Lines, Veils and the "X"

An adventuring party is only good if everybody is having a good time. A great way to make sure everyone is having fun is to make sure each person feels comfortable before the game even starts. This is where Content Warnings, Lines, and Veils come into play.

A **Content Warning** system can be used at the beginning of every session to set player expectations and allow you, the Game Runner, to make sure your team knows what they are getting themselves into. For example, Children of UMA features action movie violence, blood, guts, and gore. Starting a session by explaining, "hey buddies, just FYI, there's a little bit of chainsaw body violence in today's story. Just wanted to let you know." can let everyone be on the same page about what the story includes.

Some players may be into chainsaw body violence, while others might not be (and it's totally cool if they aren't). Others may be cool with only some of these things but not everything. You should always give everyone an opportunity to draw their lines.

Lines are just what they sound like, lines in the sand that should not be crossed. Some examples of this could be animal abuse, child death and endangerment, and sexual assault. The players should never be subjected to something that would make them feel uncomfortable or unsafe so you should always take a moment to go around the table and see what kind of lines the players wouldn't like to cross. Also be sure to let them know that it's okay if they don't want to share their lines publicly. Be sure to give everyone a way to message you offline about them before you start. Once the players declare what their lines are it is your job to make sure not to cross them. An example of this might be a player saying "I'm cool with whatever, but if the dog dies I'm gonna be super mad."

Next, ask the players for their veils. ***Veils*** are things that can be alluded to but not dwelled upon. For instance, if a player dislikes spiders and you enter a room with a massive spider-infested web you can bring it into view and then quickly pull away from it. No reason to linger on something that might upset a player.

Even after laying out lines and veils, a situation might arise where something unforeseen in the game might pop up and cause a player discomfort or distress. The best planning in the world might miss something. It's a valid player reaction and just because everyone is in the middle of the session doesn't mean they can't call attention to something. This is where the X comes into play

Players should always have the option to throw up an **X**, be it a hand signal, text in a chat, physical card, or whatever was pre- established during set up. X means stop, do not pass go, do not collect 200 dollars, and don't make a big deal about it. Just pull away from that scene immediately and move on.

Trust me when I say that taking a few minutes at the beginning of your session to make sure everybody is comfortable can almost guarantee your players will still be smiling at the end of it and looking forward to the next one.

Lines and Veils were originally developed by Ron Edwards for a piece called "Sex And Sorcery". The "X Card" was originally developed by John Stavropoulos.

Read more about them here: http://tinyurl.com/x-card-rpg

Index of Common Terms:

Band: Oxford Dictionary defines band as a "group of people who do something together or who have the same ideas, interests or achievements. A collective of individuals under one banner or leader". The Hellsings, Death Point Raiders, Black Swans, Blue Dragons, Urchins, and the Slaughter Sisters are all bands that exist within the World of Uma. We stayed away from using the word gang because the Oxford Dictionary defines gang as "an organized group of criminals," which isn't the vibe we want. We also chose not to use clan because Oxford defines it as "a group of close-knit and interrelated families" and most characters you'll meet are orphans or forgotten since the great war on the coast. They all band together to survive.

Commandeer: the act of taking over another vehicle. It takes place in two parts. The first is an Action Check to board the vehicle and the second is attacking or otherwise incapacitating the driver. It should be known that most commandeering in the game happens at full speed.

Sluice: an edible glucose runoff from solar battery charging. It can be used to sustain life or fermented into alcohol.

Vehicle: Any drivable or pilotable plane, train, or automobile. We'll use the term vehicle to cover a broad range of items capable of locomotion. Keep in mind that all players have a basic understanding of how to use each vehicle in the game.

UMA's World

Children of UMA takes place in the same universe as *Rocket to Russia* and *Point Nemo* but about 50 years in the future. Following the events of those books, **the Amphikura** - a species of fish/human hybrids - invaded every country, and a coastal war was waged. The unrelenting nature of these attacks has led to much of the world's resources being used in this war, leaving vast swaths of society forgotten.

The Hellsings' story takes place in Kansas – except it doesn't look like today's Kansas. Global warming and the staggering resources - natural and human - used to fight the Am-

phikura Wars have led to a modern-day version of the Dust Bowl.

Most food production occurs in vertical factory farms in coastal warehouses, which has left traditional rural middle-class farms mostly abandoned. Leaving the fields fallow and empty has caused massive, thousand-foot tall dust storms to loom on the horizon. They can block out the sun and spring up at a moment's notice.

The state of the world has left many families broken and a whole generation of orphans left behind. They gather in **bands**, looking out for one another and fighting over scarce resources and territory. There is an unexpected upside to this new reality. Many new military technological advancements have made their way to the wasteland, which in turn has made life a little more livable.

Your Band is called **The Hellsings** and it was started by **Croc**, an ex-enforcer for the **Black Swans**. One day he was struck by divine inspiration while listening to his favorite record by The Hellsings, a rock band from before the Amphikura Wars, he felt the call to create a new band in the wasteland – a band of wild animals reclaiming a world forgotten.

Items, Equipment, And Technology

Batteries: Most vehicles in *Children of Uma* are now powered by EVs, making them electric vehicles. The batteries themselves are organic compounds that mimic the lifeforce of a living plant and synergize perfectly with solar chargers. Because of this the batteries do repair themselves slowly and have a shelf life that extends into the decades.

Solar Charger: Solar cell chargers are now far more efficient and fold out like an origami flower. They are so efficient that they even work at night, capturing ambient moon and starlight. Using futuristic organic chemistry they not only create and charge batteries but they also make water and sluice, an edible form of glucose. The solar cells can self-repair if left in the sun, making them more durable.

Grappling Gun: -2 bonus to **Action Checks** while boarding an enemy vehicle. This pneumatic device was created for jungle combat against the Amphikura but it has since been

repurposed by bands in the wasteland to board and commandeer other bands' vehicles. It fires a light but strong line that requires **3 LP** to cut.

Cellular "Wet" Programming: Direct interface programming and hacking. Hacking can now occur by touch in certain instances and no longer require a keyboard or mouse. This is also how Elliot Tanzeer controls the Coliseum.

Carbon+ Power: High-density energy cubes have replaced fossil fuels for more significant vehicles. Larger vehicles that weigh several tons or have high demands such as flying use Carbon+.

Radio Transmitters: Every player and many NPCs have radio transmitters in their helmets to easily communicate with each other or their home bases. Unless otherwise stated, communication loops are closed so NPCs can't eavesdrop on the player's communications and vice versa.

Subsonic Attacks: Military-grade sonic weapons were initially designed as a deterrent for Amphikura and reportedly repurposed for use on civilians. Some versions can be used to influence or control the weather.

Supplemental Rules

Vehicular Combat Rules

Children of UMA features an expanded vehicular combat supplement to the standard *3,2,1...Action!* ruleset. All these rules should work seamlessly with the existing rules but if something isn't working or gelling, feel free to drop us a line or amend the rules in your own homebrew.

In-vehicle Combat: You can attack with your weapon (for example, shooting out the window) or with the vehicle's mounted or specialized weapons. You will deal damage to an opponent's vehicle first unless otherwise specified. Some weapons or special abilities can allow damage to riders directly, but these are few and far between. Use them wisely.

Luck Point Damage

Vehicles have their pool of Luck Points. These are depleted first when you are attacked or otherwise take damage. A player can also use their own pool of Luck Points to repair their vehicle at the cost of forgoing one of their two attacks per turn.

To clarify what can happen on a player's turn: they can always move and either make two attacks or one SA (special ability) or they can have one attack and spend personal Luck Points to repair their vehicle.

As the Game Runner, you might want to assist in visualizing what a Luck Point repair may look like. Here is the repair chart. Feel free to add your own or let the players improvise.

Luck Point Repair Chart

1. The player smashes their fist on the dashboard and suddenly the car repairs itself.
2. The player pats the lucky bobblehead on their dash.
3. The player grabs duct tape from the glove box and puts it to use.
4. The player uses a mini fire extinguisher to put out a fire.

Vehicular Guts Penalties

While vehicles have their own pool of Luck for physical damage caused by attacks from fire, projectiles, and weapons, each vehicle can also suffer a **Guts Penalty**. This could result from certain impact damage and other types of environmental hazards that could affect the overall bodily well-being of the vehicle.

For instance, if a vehicle rams into another vehicle resulting in a **Guts Check**, failure will result in a Guts Penalty for that vehicle. Should a vehicle receive 3 **Guts Penalties** all their stats will drop by 1. On the 4th **Guts Penalty** the vehicle is wasted.

An example of this could be the opening scene of the Road Warrior, where Mad Max performs a pit maneuver on an enemy vehicle which, in game terms, fails its 4th **Guts Check** and flips over.

Riders And Passengers

Most vehicles can have a passenger or multiple passengers. If you are a passenger in another player's vehicle you can perform your own attacks from their vehicle during your turn, such as firing your submachine gun from the back of another player's motorcycle. If the vehicle, like a Dune Buggy, has an additional attack, such as a turret or Gatling gun, you can use that during your turn.

Commandeering A Vehicle

Leaping or jumping from vehicle to vehicle at high speed is always dangerous. A player boarding a friendly vehicle must make an **Action Check +1** to avoid falling.

A player can also attempt to board an opponent's vehicle to commandeer it. They must make an **Action Check +2** for a standard vehicle or an **Action Check +3** for a heavily fortified vehicle (noted in the vehicle's description). The player can modify this roll by expending Luck Points or using certain items like a Grappling Gun.

Once the player is on board their opponent's vehicle they may directly attack the Luck Points of the vehicle's driver. When the driver's Luck Points are depleted the player has control of the vehicle.

Wasted!

A vehicle with either 0 LP or **4 Guts Penalties** is considered **Wasted!** When a ride gets wasted the driver and any passengers can either make an **Action Check +1** to jump on another player's vehicle or make an **Action Check +2** to try and commandeer a nearby enemy vehicle. The player may cause Luck Point damage to the enemy driver and once the driver is at 0 luck they are booted from their seat and the player officially takes over.

GR Notes: If a player fails their **Action Check** to jump on another vehicle they will land on the side of the road. They will barrel roll or whatever but they won't take extra damage from the fall because this is cinematic roleplaying (unless your Game Runner is mean). Another player can then pick them up on their turn and return the player to combat.

Driving & Road Hazards

Since most of the gameplay in *Children of UMA* will occur while riding in or on vehicles the Player and Game Runner should treat the movement as normal, requiring no roll for basic movement, even at top speed. If you are maneuvering around the battlefield and there are no **Road Hazards** present you are able to do so freely and without penalty.

While many would imagine a road hazard as a downed tree or a large pothole, a road hazard in Children of UMA could be considered anything that would inhibit how a person would normally drive their vehicle. It can be hard to drive in a straight line when the ground is crumbling or you are pinned between a semi and a ridge on a sharp left turn. For anything other than driving in a straight line on a flat road the GR may add a bonus or penalty.

GR Notes: Since this is a post-apocalyptic driving adventure all cars will be considered to be driving at top speed while in pursuit.

Road Hazards: If a Game Runner wants to spice up an encounter or add a complication roll 1d10 on the chart below.

1. Fire
2. Dust Bowl Twister
3. Wildling Attack (aka The Hills Have Eyes).
4. Amphikura Attack
5. Old man in an M2 Bradley (Tank Daddy)
6. Minor Earthquake
7. Lightning Storm
8. Wasted old cars are left on the road
9. Oil Slick
10. Unfinished Segment of Highway

Optional Rules

Back Me Up

Should the players find themselves with too few vehicles between scenes, the GR could, at their discretion, introduce another vehicle to the players. This could be done by having Croc loan the players his prized Trans Am or having Crow and Fox show up in a tow truck with a few motorcycles in the back. Either way use this rule sparingly to keep the players trying to commandeer new rides for themselves.

Hardcore Vehicle Mode

Your starting vehicles are what you get. You can repair or "take what's yours" by commandeering enemy vehicles, but you do not get the between-episode vehicle refresh.

Sample Play Session

Here is a sample play session to give you an idea of how the *Children of Uma* could be run. It could be adjusted depending on your group's playing style or desires.

The Game Runner: It's 6:45 in the morning and the sun has already begun to rise in the east, though not yet piercing the dust clouds on the plains. It is unseasonably hot for this time of year and you can feel the sweat pooling on your lower back. Thankfully the cooling system in your helmet keeps your head dry. In the distance you hear the sound of rhythmic thunder. The ground shakes beneath you and within moments the Death Pont Raiders' caravan is barreling down Route 21. You see your target, a Semi Truck containing the supplies you need to keep your camp going, and behind it ride several bikers, a school bus, and what looks like a bunch of speakers on wheels. It's hard to tell because it goes by in a flash. You hear a crackle in your helmet and then Croc's voice breaks through, "It's time."

As you pull onto the highway you find yourself at the tail end of the caravan behind two Dweebs on Dirt Bikes with submachine guns dangling from shoulder straps. The Death Point Raiders' mobile barracks are within two cars' distance ahead of them. The sound of multiple vehicles and whatever is causing that rhythmic thunder has masked the sound of your vehicles. Because of this you'll have the element of surprise on your side for the first turn of combat.

Alright Hellsings, it's time for some Action! Take a couple of minutes and figure out your plan and when you are ready, let me know what's the play?

Combat Turn 1: The GR asks the players what they would like to do. This is a great opportunity to encourage the players to devise a plan where they can work together or separately and remind them that this is a cinematic storytelling adventure so anything goes. Once the GR has everyone's basic actions figured out they will make the players roll. The GR calculates the rolls and plays out the scene with whatever successes or failures occur. This can require a degree of improvisation on the GR's part. Here is how that might look like:

Barney: Well, Owl is in the back of the Dune Buggy on the harpoon gun, but I have my drone that can drop control pods. I want to use it to drop a pod onto the bus and try to take control on my next turn.

Amir: Dog is driving the Dune Buggy. I want to try and use the Overdrive Special Ability to try and run over one of the motorcycles.

Bea: Cat is piloting the Gyrocopter. I want to fly to the Mobile Barracks and strafe bullets at it.

Gwen: Bat is hanging from the Gyrocopter's winch. While Cat is flying by I want to dive off the Gyrocopter and use my wingsuit to glide over to the top of the barracks.

Cassie: Rat is driving the Ripper ATV. I want to ride up on the right side of the Mobile

Barracks and use the Rolling Chainsaw Special Ability and try to slash at its tires.

The Game Runner: Alright, Cassie roll your damage for the attack.

Cassie: 11

The Game Runner: Awesome! Amir Make an **Action Check +2** for me.

Amir: 9. Crap.

The Game Runner: Do you want to spend some **Luck Points** to succeed?

Amir: Yes.

The Game Runner: Badass. Barney, make your **Action Check** for your drone. Gwen you get a bonus for the wingsuit so just a +1 for your **Action Check**.

Barney & Gwen: Made it!

The Game Runner: Okay, so here is how this goes down. Owl starts tapping away on her wrist-mounted keypad and flies off into the sky unseen. It drops the pod onto the bus's hood and veers off to the west to return to your next turn. Dog kicks the Dune Buggy into overdrive and jerks the steering wheel hard, which causes the Buggy's oversized tires to roll right over the first dirt bike. It crushes the bike and kills the Dweeb rider dead. Cat strafes to the left side of the bus, flying low and shooting out the windows. You see Dweebs hit the decks. While this is happening, Bat silently glides and lands on the roof. The chaos conceals the sound of her boots landing. Rat rolls up on the right side of the bus, chainsaw blades roaring. You notice the back of the bus is on treads instead of tires. The ripper still does damage but you spot that you've got bigger problems ahead. There is a Dweeb-controlled turret with a massive cannon that is now turning 180 degrees in your direction. Now it's my turn.

Cassie: Oh, shit.

Combat Turn 2: This is the enemy reaction round. In *3,2,1...Action!* the players generally go first and then the enemy goes.

The Game Runner: Okay, let me make a few rolls. Starting at the back of the bus the remaining Dweeb on a motorcycle steers his bike towards the Dune Buggy and successfully leaps to the right front side, shadowing Dog as his bike slides backwards on the hot asphalt and making a terrible screeching noise. He will try and commandeer the buggy next turn.

The backdoor and roof hatch of the school bus both pop open at the same time. Cutting through the full throttle thunder you hear an angry chorus of Dweebs as two on mini bikes launch out of the back of the bus. They're going to be in combat on the Raiders' next turn. Two more Dweebs start hurling trash onto the road; orange cones, old microwaves, pots, pans, stop signs and bags of garbage, creating a road hazard. Amir, make an **Action Check +2** for me as you are about to drive over the debris.

Amir: I have a -1 bonus to **Action Checks** when driving over road hazards because of the Dune Buggy, so it'll just be an **Action Check +1**. Made it!

Barney: Do I have to roll anything?

The Game Runner: Nope, you are good Barn! Amir's got the wheel so only he has to make the check. So while this is happening, two more Dweebs with rifles pop out of the roof hatch. One immediately starts firing on the Gyrocopter and the other at Bat! The Gyrocopter takes **7 Luck Points** damage while the first shot at Bat misses by a yard. The second shot is but a flesh wound for **1 Luck Point**.

Gwen: That son of a bitch must pay!

Bea: It's fine.

The Game Runner: Hahaha, and finally Rat. The turret finally makes its 180-degree turn in your direction and it struggles to make the shot as the bus driver jerks the wheel to the left to maneuver away from the Gyrocopter's bullets. The blast still hits your ATV and does 8 Luck Points damage. Can you make a **Guts Check** for me?

Cassie: Failed it.

The Game Runner: Do you want to spend any Luck?

Cassie: Nope, I got a plan.

The Game Runner: Alright, so in addition to the **8 Luck Points** damage the ATV will also take 1 **Guts Penalty**. The two Dweebs on Mini Bikes are looping back around. One unfurls a chain and starts whipping it around his head while the other pulls out a molotov cocktail and lights it. They rev their motors and start heading towards the Dune Buggy. It's the players' turn now.

Combat Turn 3: The GR repeats all the same steps they did in turn 1.

Bea: I can handle the Mini Bikes, Gwen. Can you take out one of the Dweebs? I think I can get the other one too.

Gwen: No problem!

Amir: If you've got the Mini Bikes, Bea, I want to try and take out the Dweeb on my Buggy. Barney, will you use the Control Pod or would you be down to shoot the Harpoon gun at the turret if I swing us by?

Barney: Yo, let's take out that turret.

Bea: Got you covered on the Mini Bikes, Amir.

Cassie: I've got a plan so crazy it just might not get me killed!

The Game Runner: Hell yeah. Okay, so let's go down the line starting with you, Bea.

Bea: Okay, I want to strafe around and open fire at the Dweeb closest to the end of the bus and the two Mini Bikes.

Gwen: I want to baseball slide under the Dweeb who shot me and use my Quick-blades' Sneak Attack special ability.

Amir: I want to peek over my shoulder without fully looking back and blast the Dweeb at point blank range with my shotgun.

The Game Runner: You have the Hasselblaster, so are you firing three shots with a damage bonus, right?

Amir: Damn right I am!

The Game Runner: I am still going to make you roll damage anyways, out of sheer comedy, but safe to say he's very, very dead. So Cassie, what is this crazy plan? Thrill me.

Cassie: I am going to hit the brakes and let the bus continue to go forward. When it is at a good distance, I am going to gun it and drive full speed at the bus. At the last second I slam on my breaks, launching myself over the handlebars at the open back door. I want to somersault in as I draw both handguns and open fire.

The Players: WHAAAAAAAAAAT?!?! Hahahahahahahah!

The Game Runner: Hahaha wow. Oh wow. I need a minute.

Cassie: Told ya. Rat is a wildcard.

The Game Runner: Cassie, make an **Action Check +3** to attempt this stunt or Fill The Plot Hole In Two Sentences. How are you so acrobatic?

Cassie: When I was growing up at the camp, Bear started teaching a class called Tumblin' For Lil' Tumblers. She taught the younglings how to safely roll out of a moving vehicle and other acrobatic exercises. I was her best student and never stopped tumblin'.

The Game Runner: Great, make it an **Action Check +1**

Cassie: Made it.

The Game Runner: Holy Crap, hahaha. Roll damage for two attacks.

Cassie: 13

The Game Runner: Gwen, Barney, Bea, and Amir roll damage.

Amir: 23 points of damage to the Dweeb!

The Game Runner: Sweet Christmas! That Dweeb's entire bloodline felt that shot. Woof.

Bea: 12

Gwen: 9

Barney: 10

The Game Runner: Nice damage, everybody. Alright Hellsings, here's the finish.

Cat swings the Gyrocopter around and angles forward, shooting the Dweeb who fired at her off the roof. You can faintly hear a Wilhelm scream as he plummets off the side of the bus to his death. The rest of the bullets had the Molotov Dweebs' name on them because as he is peppered with hot lead his arm jerks wildly and he loosens his grip on the Molotov Cocktail. It spins through the air, accidentally lands on his cohort and engulfs him in flames. His riding gloves mold onto his hand grips as they melt and he slowly drifts off the road, ablaze. The other Dweeb on the roof takes his eyes off Bat for a moment in the chaos but that's all she needs. Bat slides up behind him and pierces his heart with her Quickblade, killing him before he can exhale.

Dog whispers into his helmet headset, "I got this, Owl! Get the harpoon ready!". Without taking his eyes off the road he aims his Hasselblaster over his right shoulder and fires. The gun explodes the Dweeb's head, launching his body back and raining blood down on Owl. The body doesn't make it too far and is immediately impaled on the harpoon, unconsciously deciding turnabout is fair play and spurting blood all over Dog. Dog races forward and banks towards the right side of the bus giving Owl a clear shot at the turret. Owl wipes the blood away from his visor and fires. The harpoon flies a little slower because there is a headless Dweeb attached but it connects with the turret. From the front seat Dog can see the Turret Dweeb projectile vomiting all over the turret bubble.

Rat pumps the brakes and the bus and the Dune Buggy fly past. She hits top speed in pursuit and when she gets close enough she slams on the brakes. The Ripper ATV bucks forward, launching Rat headfirst over the handlebars into the bus's open door. She pulls her entire body in tight as she turns mid-air into the back of the bus. When she hits the ground the muscle memory from the tumbling training she got as a small child kicks in and she gracefully returns to her feet, guns drawn, and unleashes hell upon the Dweebs, killing the driver instantly.

His lifeless body slumps over the wheel as his foot releases from the gas. The bus starts to slow before it ultimately comes to a stop. The rest of the Dweebs raise their hands in surrender, knowing they are outmatched.

The End?

Playable Characters

The Hellsings

Hellsings Dog - Aki - "The Muscle"

Age 14. Lawrence, Kansas. He/Him

Aki was always the biggest kid growing up which made him a target, especially with older kids. He quickly learned how to defend himself despite how much he abhors violence. While he carries a shotgun for necessity, he favors knocking out opponents with his Power Glove, which he designed and maintained.

Starting Inventory: Power Glove, **Shotgun**

Power Glove: When activated, the Power Glove gives its wearer a -2 to **Action** and **Brawn Checks**.

Special Ability: GTS (Go to Sleep): Instead of making an attack, Dog can use the Power Glove to release a "knock out" gas that puts their opponent to sleep for three turns or until they are attacked. When commandeering a vehicle, the player may use this Special Ability to stun the vehicle's driver forcing them to make a **Guts Check +3** or be launched from the vehicle, freeing up the driver seat for the player.

25 LP	
Action 6	Cool 4
Brains 5	Charm 6
Brawn 7	Guts 6

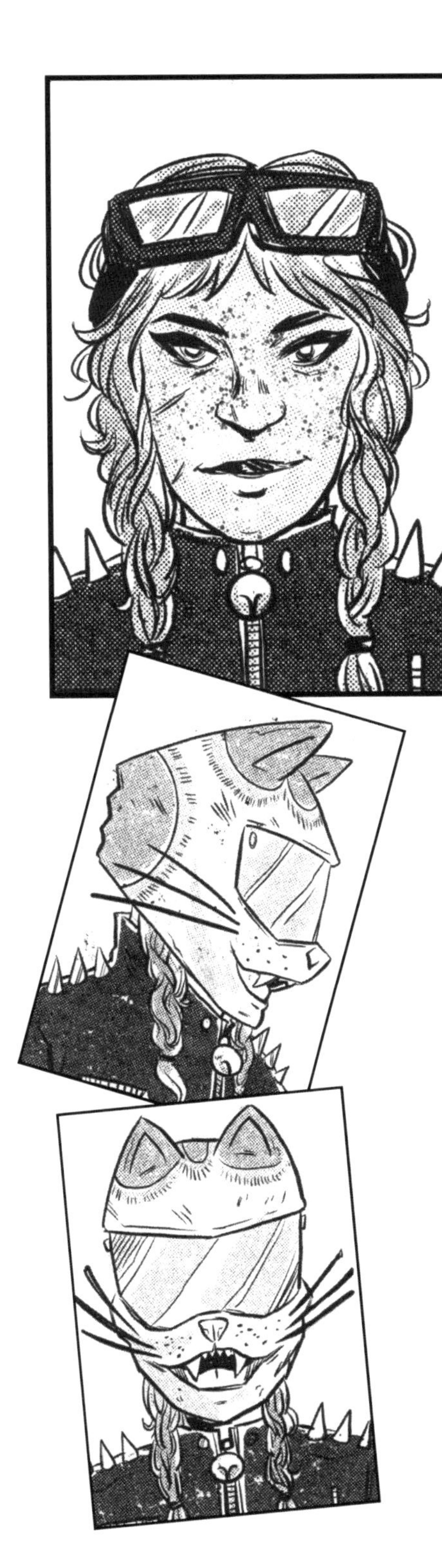

Hellsings Cat - Cattie - Mechanic
Age 16. Belleville, Kansas. She/Her

Cattie's got a lot of energy and can't stand being still. She was a mechanic's apprentice who worked on Croc's bike when he was in the Black Swans. She was also one of the first people he recruited into the Hellsings when he found out the Black Swans would punish her for cannibalizing parts to work on her secret projects.

Starting Inventory: Bandolier Tool-Kit, Hydrospanner, **Shock Baton**, Cheetos

GR Notes: Cat's pet Prairie Dog, Squeegee, does not take up an inventory slot. Cheetos are his favorite snack.

Special Ability: Nine Lives: On her turn, Cat can restore 2 Luck Points for every 1 she sacrifices to repair the vehicle she's driving. She may also remove 1 **Guts Penalty** from any vehicle she is riding in.

23 LP	
Action 7	Cool 6
Brains 6	Charm 5
Brawn 4	Guts 4

Squeegee - Superintelligent Pet

1ft tall, 3lbs. Age 3, A secret research facility called "The Warren."

One night while charging her bike under the stars Cat heard something in the brush. When she went to investigate she found what looked like a large prairie dog with a lion mane stuck in a steel trap. She grabbed her tin snips and cut him loose. Squeegee hasn't left her side since, always bringing her snacks or prizes whenever he goes off on one of his quests.

Special Ability: Indestructible : Should any perceived mortal harm befall Squeegee, he will just exit the scene and reappear magically in the next one.

∞ LP	
Action 7	Cool 5
Brains 7	Charm 8
Brawn 2	Guts 2

Hellsings Rat - Rodge: Rogue

Age 12, Parts Unknown. They/Them

Rodge just mysteriously showed up one day at the Hellsing camp and nobody has questioned where they came from, whether they belonged, or what their story was. Croc liked something about them right out the gate so they were allowed to stay in the group.

Starting Inventory: Grappling Gun (-2 bonus to **Action Checks** when commandeering), Lockpicks (-1 bonus to **Brains Checks** while picking locks), **Submachine Gun, Quick Blade**

Special Ability: Stab Your Back!: On her turn, while using a bladed weapon, Rat may make an **Action Check +1** to sneak up on a target and attack. If successful, Rat's attack will do double the damage. If she doesn't kill her opponent outright they will immediately make a counterattack at DMG 0.

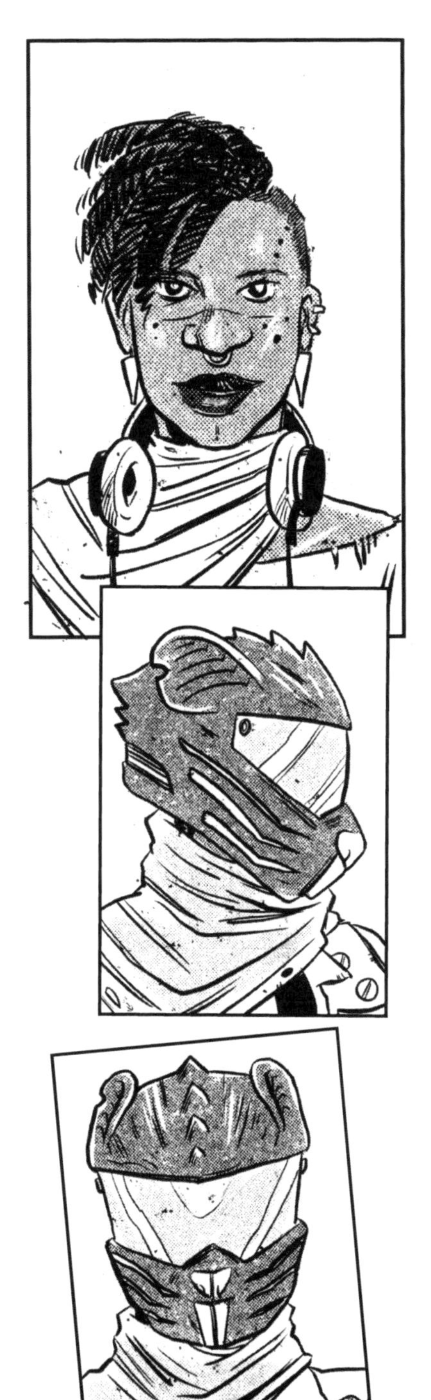

22 LP	
Action 8	Cool 7
Brains 6	Charm 4
Brawn 4	Guts 5

Hellsings Bat - Alexis: Spy

Age 13, Belleville, Kansas. She/Her

Alexis is Cat's little sister and, just like her older sister, has way too much energy. Where Cat keeps herself focused on mechanical things, Bat's focus has always been on finding her next adrenaline fix. Her favorite pastime is finding high-up places no one else would dare go and then jumping off them.

Starting Inventory: Wingsuit (-1 bonus to **Action Checks** for airborne commandeering), Morbius Brick, **Handgun (2)**

Special Ability - Energy Vampire: Instead of attacking, Bat may use her wingsuit to fly over to an enemy vehicle and drain up to 5 of its Luck Points using her Morbius Brick. Once drained, Bat may keep these Luck Points in reserve for her next vehicle or make an **Action Check +1** to fly over to one of her teammates' vehicles and top them off with the Luck Points.

Roll 1d10 for Luck Point Drain:

1 = **1**/2,3 = **2**/4,5,6 = **3**/7,8,9 = **4**/10 = **5**

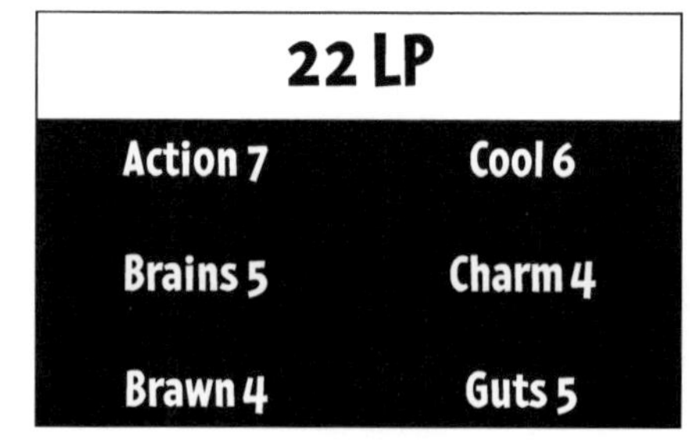

22 LP	
Action 7	Cool 6
Brains 5	Charm 4
Brawn 4	Guts 5

Helsings Owl - Jaq: Programmer

Age 14, Wichita, Kansas. She/Her

Puzzle solving and hacking have always been second nature to Jaq. Both her parents worked at a military research facility and Jaq used to try and help them in the computer lab. The facility was destroyed by an Ampfikura raid and Jaq was one of the few survivors. Sent to live with her uncle in Kansas, everything was fine until he got caught up in an altercation between a now extinct band called the Iron Horses and the Black Swans. Croc took her in as a member of the Hellsings. She is now fiercely protective of her new family.

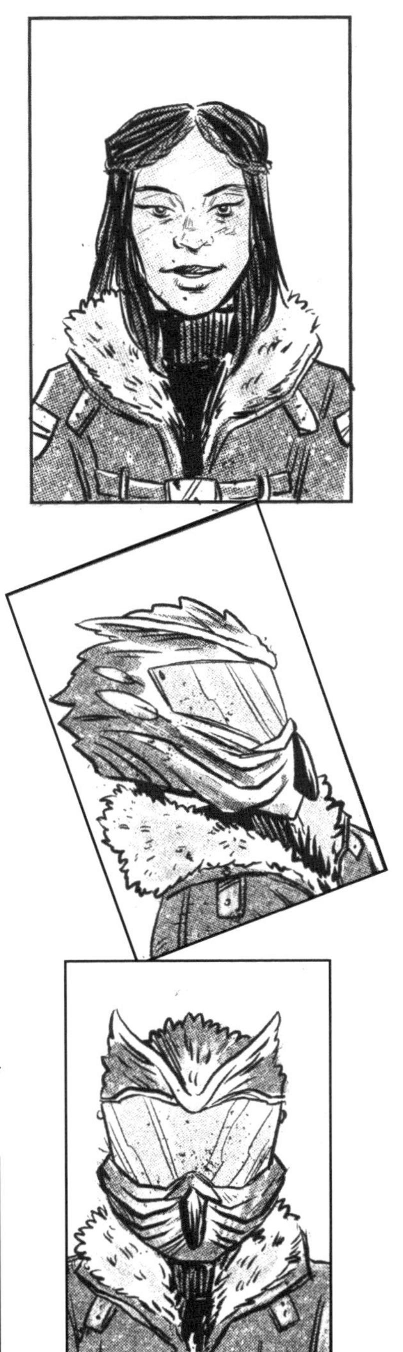

Starting Inventory: Wrist Keypad, Drone, 3 Sticky Pods (for remote commandeering), **Sub Machine Gun**

Drone: This wrist keypad-controlled airborne drone can drop Owl's Sticky Pods onto enemy vehicles and use them to hack and control that vehicle later. Owl can sacrifice one attack to make an **Action Check +1** to fly her drone over an enemy vehicle and drop a sticky pod.

Special Ability: Possession: Once Owl's drone attaches a Sticky Pod to an enemy vehicle, Owl may forgo her attack to make a **Brains Check** and take over the vehicle's controls and do one of three things.

1) Brains Check +1 - Kill the engine on a motorcycle-sized vehicle for one turn.

2) Brains Check +2 - Steer a car-sized vehicle for one turn.

3) Brains Check +3 - Control the weapons system of a larger vehicle for one turn.

23 LP	
Action 6	Cool 5
Brains 7	Charm 3
Brawn 4	Guts 4

Helsings Hare - "Magic Man"
Age 12, Garden City, Kansas. He/Him

Hare signed up for the military because he wanted to be like his older brother. A misfired experiment bomb during basic training accidentally wiped out his entire platoon. After the carnage Hare popped his head out of a fox hole he had found himself in and decided army life wasn't for him. He made his way from the coast back to his home state of Kansas, one hitchhike at a time.

Starting Inventory: Deck of playing cards, Flash Paper, **Magnet Hatchets**, **Sub Machine Gun**

Special Ability: "Just Lucky, I Guess": Should Hare drop to 0 LP, once per episode, he may appear as if by magic on one of his teammate's vehicles with 1 LP so long as he can explain how he got there using two sentences or less and ending the story with "just lucky, I guess."

24 LP	
Action 8	Cool 4
Brains 5	Charm 6
Brawn 5	Guts 5

Hellsings Croc: Leader of the Hellsings
Age 18, Dodge City, Kansas. He/Him

When you are young, tough, and alone, the Black Swan is a great place to be. Croc spent a few years dressed in the black doing missions for Mrs. Olivia, trying to maintain peace in the Midwest. He was professional and quickly rose to the ranks, becoming one of her favorite lieutenants. But after years of grinding, Croc felt lost in the brutal bureaucracy of the Black Swans. That was when he came across an old vinyl record on a raiding mission which changed everything for him.

Starting Inventory: Hasselblaster

Special Ability: "Business In The Front, Party In The Back": Croc has a totally sweet mullet, and we all know any person willing to rock a mullet is fully committed to the life and not one to take lightly. Once per scene, Croc may use his special ability to assist his squad.

Business Up Front: Rally the troops giving them all a -2 Bonus to their current Check.

Party In The Back: If one of his team is feeling the heat, he can chill them out, removing **1 Guts Penalty.**

GR Notes: Croc has a -2 damage reduction due to his hardened skin from his shot of UMA.

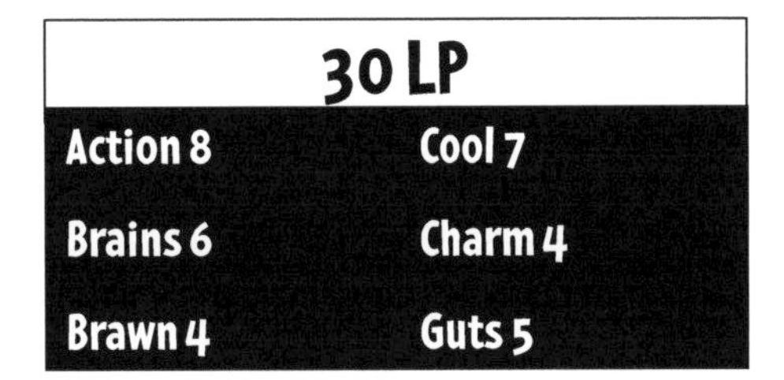

30 LP	
Action 8	Cool 7
Brains 6	Charm 4
Brawn 4	Guts 5

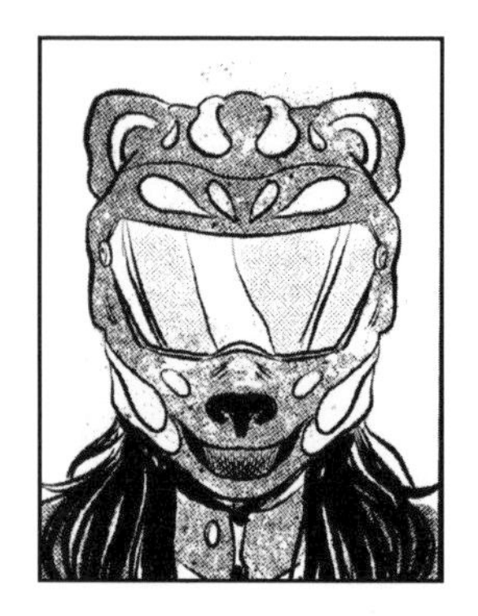

Hellsings Bear - Age 21

Bear is the Hellsing's mechanic, repairer, and tinkerer. In her younger years, she was a bit of a hellcat and ended up losing her leg in a race. Now slightly older (21 is middle age in the wasteland) she tries her best to help others from being as reckless as she was.

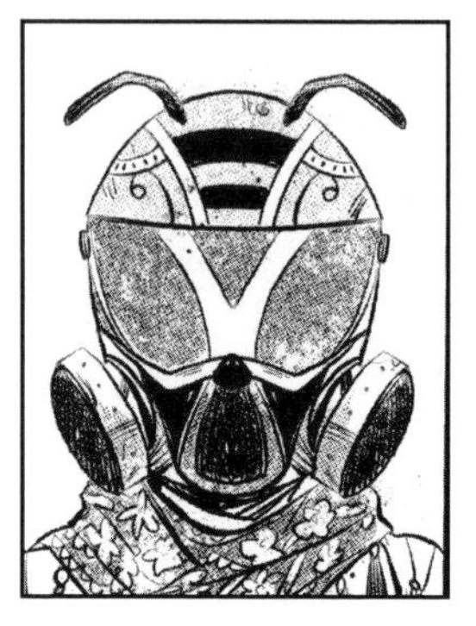

Hellsings Bee - Age 22

In another life, Bee would have been an amazing grammar school teacher but that world is long gone. Now Bee spends his days ensuring the Hellsings are fed and taken care of. The dust storms exacerbate his asthma, but he always makes sure the Hellsings are ready for action.

Hellsings Wolf - Hellsings Lieutenant, Age 17

Wolf was the best scout the Hellsing's ever had. She was Croc's most trusted confidant and he valued her insights and opinions over his own. She recruited the most Hellsings after Croc and always looked after her pack, ferociously attacked anyone who messed with them. She also personally recruited Aki.

Hellsings Crow - Age 15

You'll usually find Crow in his glider. High up in the sky, he jots down notes about band movements and other information he finds in an old composition notebook. Rumors are that Crow can smell death and his intuition has saved the Hellsings more than once.

Hellsings Fox - Age 12

Fox grew up in the skeletal ruins of the inner city. She is the most adept at thriving in that concrete and steel landscape. Climbing fire escapes and making her way rooftop to rooftop, it's the only place Fox feels truly free.

Hellsings Cub - Age 13

Impressionable and eager, Cub can be found either helping Boar blow up random bits of junk or helping Bear fix and build vehicles. Either way, he tries his best but doesn't always have a solid barometer for making good choices.

Hellsings Boar - Age 19

Whether welding new weapons or trying to devise new and interesting ways of blowing things up, Boar is the loud and brash Hellsings weaponsmith and demolitions expert. Despite being elbow deep in gunpowder, he likes to show off his artistic side and designed the band's signature helmets.

Hellsings Playable Rides

The wasteland doesn't always provide access to the newest vehicles but here are some basic rides everyone can utilize. Bear or Cat can add different mods to vehicles once they are unlocked.

Dirt Bike (Battery-Powered)

7ft Length, 3ft Width, 3ft Height, 220lbs., One Rider / 3 Upgrade Slots

Description: This is your standard late 2050s Dirt Bike, the kind all of the cool metal-heads your mom warned you about used to ride in the woods behind the Grammar School. It's battery-powered and tricked out with dual machine guns attached to its front fork.

2 Attacks or 1 SA Per Turn

Kick/Punch: MV 5ft DMG -6

Special Ability - Hard to Kill: While weaving in and out of traffic the rider can get one attack against another vehicle from any direction. Using this SA will also grant them a -1 Luck Point damage reduction on their next turn, as they will be harder to hit while performing this ability.

Specail Ability - Ghost Rider: With a successful **Action Check**, you can board any large vehicle (like a Semi-truck or Cargo Train) while your bike will "ghost ride" alongside and be available whenever you choose to exit. Unless someone else takes it, that is

20 LP		
Action 8	**Brawn 3**	**Charm -**
Brains -	**Cool -**	**Guts 4**

Ripper ATV (Battery-Powered)

6ft Length 4ft Width, 4ft Height, 420lbs., One Rider / 3 Upgrade Slots

Description: This four-wheel ATV is battery-powered and good for both on and off-road riding. Wrapped around the outside of the ATV is a saw-toothed track, designed by Bishop Motorsports as a homage to owner Bob Bishop's favorite movie, "The Texas Chainsaw Massacre". This track enables the Ripper to attack enemy vehicles on all sides as well as spin the teeth around the outer track creating a rolling chainsaw effect.

2 Attacks or 1 SA Per Turn

The Ripper: DMG -5 The Ripper can use jagged steel barbs to cut into the side panels of their opponent's vehicles causing them external damage and forcing some breathing room between the rider and their foes.

Special Ability - Buzzkill: 3 Uses, DMG 0 Jagged steel barbs wrap around the ATV on a chain and spin in 360 degrees to slice and slash its opponent's vehicles with its sharp edges while also protecting the rider from their foes. The Buzzkill may be used against multiple vehicles at the same time but will be rendered inoperable after the third use.

20 LP		
Action 7	**Brawn 6**	**Charm -**
Brains -	**Cool**	**Guts 5**

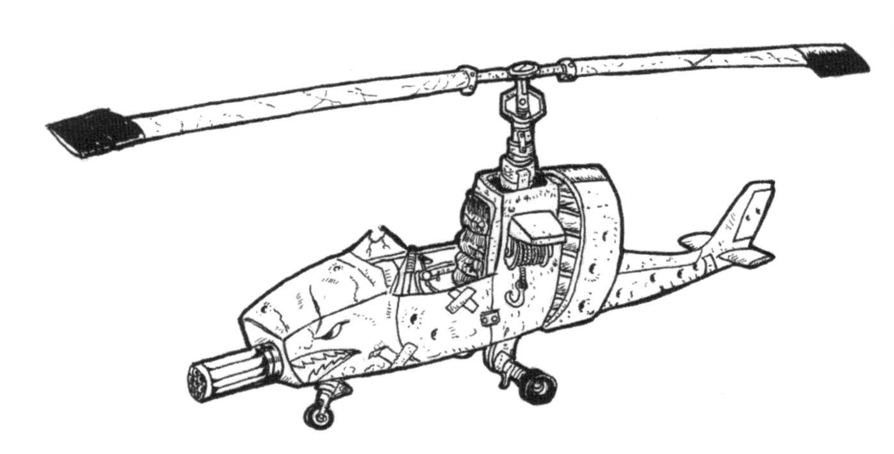

Gyrocopter (Carbon Plus Powered)

16 ft Length, 6ft Width, 9ft Height, 584lbs., One Rider, One Hanger-On / 2 Upgrade Slots

Description: This single-passenger Carbon+ powered Gyrocopter may look as if it was held together by a wish and a prayer but has gotten the team out of more scrapes than a good lawyer and money ever could. Its maneuverability at lower and higher altitudes makes the Gyrocopter the perfect support vehicle.

2 Attacks or 1 SA Per Turn

Gatling Gun: 200 Round Cartridge, DMG -2 The pilot will gently squeeze the trigger of the Gatling to release a controlled burst at their foes.

GR Notes: The Gatling gun is more of a cinematic weapon, so while it is said to have a 200-round cartridge it is at your discretion whether you want to make the player count their bullets.

Drag & Drop: The Gyrocopter has a winch and a pulley it may use to pick up and carry a teammate to be dropped off at any point on the battlefield. This may be combined with any standard or special attack.

Special Ability - Ammo Dump: Once per turn, the Gyrocopter can hover over one of their teammates and perform an ammo drop equal to one full magazine for any gun while making a single standard attack.

Special Ability - Bullet Straffe: Will swoop in for an attack every other turn, fully pulling on the Gatling gun trigger and dealing 6 LP damage to all foes unless they can make a successful **Action Check +2** to dodge.

35 LP		
Action 7	Brawn 4	Charm -
Brains -	Cool -	Guts 4

Dune Buggy (Battery-Powered)

13ft Length, 6ft Width, 7ft Height, 555lbs., Two Riders / 3 Upgrade Slots

Description: This furious four-wheeler bounces about the battlefield, becoming harder to hit by the bullets of its foes. Unlike most Hellsings vehicles, this battery-powered buggy is built for two and ready to handle the road ahead or whatever is in the rearview!

1 Attack + 1 SA Per Turn: Driver And Passenger

Forward Rifle: 15 Round Magazine, DMG -2, Driver operated.

Special Ability - Rear Turret Harpoon Gun: 3 Harpoons, DMG 0, Passenger operated. This Harpoon Gun packs a high pressure wallop and will cause any vehicle it hits to take **1 Guts Penalty** in addition to damage.

Special Ability - Overdrive: Instead of attacking with its weapons the Buggy may make an **Action Check +2** to hop up and drive over any smaller vehicle, doing +2 damage and 1**Guts Penalty**, as well as causing that vehicle to lose one turn. For example, imagine there is a road hazard that could act as a ramp. In that case the Buggy may make an **Action Check +3** to use it as a jump, giving it the ability to launch itself onto a larger vehicle doing +3 damage as well as 1 **Guts Penalty** for both the opponent vehicle and the Buggy itself before driving away.

Special Ability - Off-Road: While driving off-road or on difficult terrain, the Dune Buggy will receive a -1 bonus to **Action Checks** and a -1 reduction to all damage rolls against it on its enemy's next turn since it will become harder to hit.

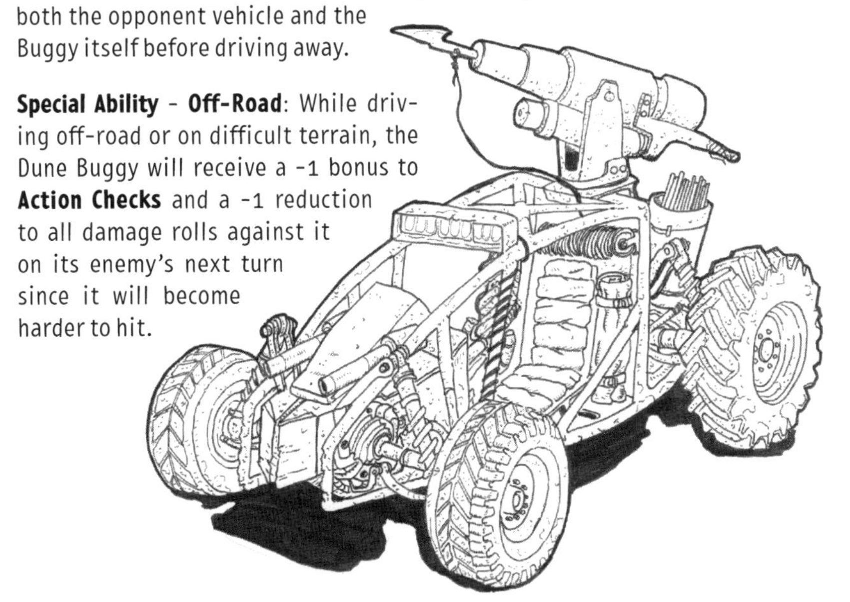

25 LP		
Action 6	**Brawn 5**	**Charm -**
Brains -	**Cool -**	**Guts 6**

Trans Am (Battery Powered)

16ft Length, 6ft Width, 4ft Height, 3,530lbs

30 LP - Two Riders / 3 Upgrade Slots

Description: Croc's pride and joy, this 2027 Smokey and the Bandit 50th Anniversary Edition Trans Am was manufactured as a limited edition with only 7,700 made. Croc found the car covered and in pristine shape, tucked away in a suburban garage on a supply run.

This T-Topped terror is metallic flake cherry red with gold trim and has the Hellsings logo in place of the firebird on the hood. This Trans Am has been upgraded with a full carbon+ powered motor, which has made the car lighter and faster.

Unlike most wasteland rides, Croc wanted his car to stand out among all the barbed wire and spikes so he tricked out the undercarriage and let the speed do the talking.

2 Attacks or 1 SA Per Turn

Specail Ability - Smokey: (One Use) This smoke screen assault will result in a +1 penalty to **Action Checks** to any vehicles caught inside of it and a -1 damage reduction to whoever is driving in front of it.

Special Ability - Bandit: (One Use) This oil slick assault will result in a +2 penalty to **Action Checks** to whoever drives through it. If conditions are right it will also light on fire, causing +3 damage and an additional 5 Luck Point damage every turn until it is extinguished or the vehicle is wasted.

Special Ability - Eastbound And Down: This legendary maneuver, perfected in the 1970s by bootleggers transporting beer from Texarkana to Atlanta, was meant to distract the local highway patrol with flashy driving while the truckers passed unseen. In the wasteland, this trick draws the enemy's attention, granting the driver a -2 damage reduction and a +2 to **Action Checks** and giving their teammates a +1 bonus to damage on their next attack.

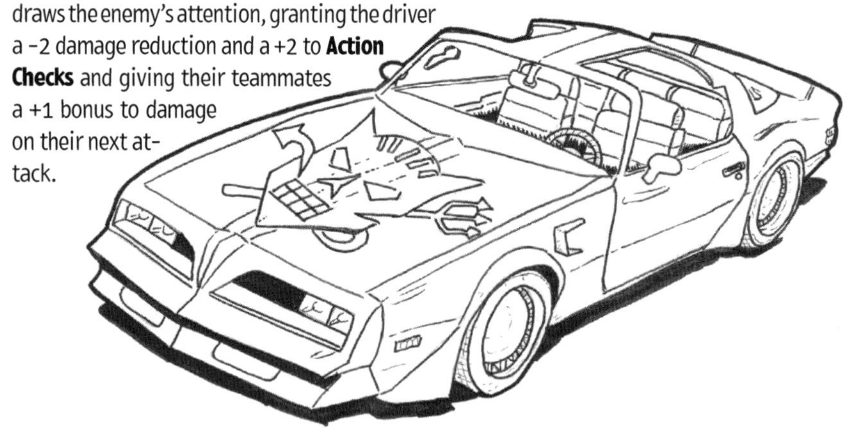

30 LP		
Action 8	**Brawn 5**	**Charm -**
Brains -	**Cool -**	**Guts 5**

Bands of the Bowl:

Here is a little history of each band, how they interact, and their general hierarchy.

DEATH POINT RAIDERS

Resolv corp hired Scorp for some paramilitary operations dealing with Amphikura on the front lines. He was cool with that. He wasn't so cool when they dragged him to the midwest to maintain order among the citizens. Unhappy, Scorp formed the Death Point Raiders and used his understanding of PSYOPS to incorporate intimidation in the form of The Music Man. He lets his lieutenant, the Naa Zaa, create an almost mystical appeal to the Death Point Raiders which led them to become one of the biggest bands and a direct threat to the Black Swans.

Dweeb: "The Cannon Fodder"

Ages 18-27, Any Pronouns

"Dweeb" is the term unaffectionately used to describe the general conscripts to the Death Point Raiders. Dweebs are considered to be highly expendable and will only achieve name status after surviving no less than five battles.

Starting Inventory: Chains, Sub Machine Gun

Special Ability - Meat Shield: Since the Dweebs who start their "careers" on the frontline are seen as "single-use", their presence grants any higher ranking Dweeb a -1 damage reduction.

1 LP
Action 5
Brains 5
Brawn 4
Cool 2
Charm 2
Guts 4

Muscle Dweeb: "The Jobber"

Ages 18-27, Any Pronouns

10 LP
Action 6
Brains 4
Brawn 7
Cool 4
Charm 5
Guts 7

While "Muscle Dweeb" may be a step up from your standard Dweeb, it is the only named non-ranking position in the Death Point Raiders. This is mostly because the Muscle Dweebs spend too much time working on their gains and not enough time working on their brains. They also say "Bro" way too much for anybody's liking.

Starting Inventory: **Submachine Gun**, Wraparound Sunglasses

Special Ability - "Do You Even Lift, Bro?": When commandeering a vehicle, a Muscle Dweeb can eject its driver by making a successful **Brawn Check +1**

Copter Dweeb: "The Pilot"

Ages 18-27, Any Pronouns

7 LP
Action 7
Brains 6
Brawn 5
Cool 4
Charm 4
Guts 5

"Copter Dweebs" are the first Dweebs of rank since they have a specific function and value to the Death Point Raiders. With that said, several Copter Dweebs in the past have risen even higher in the ranks (one of them even became Scorp's Lieutenant!). Oddly enough, the Copter Dweebs don't generally last too long in their position and often meet mysterious ends off the battlefield.

Starting Inventory: Handgun, Roll Up Tool Kit

Special Ability - Mr. Fix It: Can forgo an attack and restore 3 LP to the vehicle they are currently occupying as either a driver or rider without sacrificing Luck Points.

Sneaky Dweeb: "The Sniper"

Ages 18-27, Any Pronouns

6 LP
Action 7
Brains 6
Brawn 4
Cool 9
Charm 3
Guts 5

"Sneaky Dweebs" are considered to be the highest level of Dweeb one can attain. By rights, they should always be considered first above the rest of their compatriots for a command position. However, Scorp stopped offering promotions because they always decline. Sneaky Dweebs don't care much for rank or micro-management, preferring to get their marching orders and be left to their own devices.

Starting Inventory: Quick Blade, 50ft Rope, **Sniper Rifle**

Special Ability - Death's Whisper: Once per scene, Sneaky Dweebs can forgo an attack to completely conceal their location and, on their next turn, make a single shot at 0 DMG without revealing their position.

The Music Man: Independent Contractor

Age 27, Chicago, Illinois. He/Him

The Music Man spent his younger days learning wet programming and was eventually hired as a contractor for the military. His passion for music led him to focus on sonic weaponry. Today, he is enamored with Scorp's vision for the future and focuses his energy on making sure the Death Point Raider succeeds in their mission.

Starting Inventory: Handgun, Headphones

Special Ability - No Guest List, No Requests: The Music Man doesn't care much for clout chasers and even less for people who think their song needs to interrupt his well-curated set list. Once per turn, when a player attempts to gain access to his stage, the Music Man may eject them by throwing them off the top of La Grange onto the approaching vehicle. The player may make a **Brawn Check +3** to attempt to break his hold but if they fail they go over the edge aimed at the nearest ground vehicle while taking DMG 0 as well as **2 Guts Penalties.**

Their body will do DMG 0 to the vehicle they land on and result in a **Guts Penalty** for the vehicle as well as a +1 penalty to the player and vehicle's next **Action Check.**

25 LP
Action 6
Brains 5
Brawn 4
Cool 5
Charm 7
Guts 4

Death Heads: The Music Man's Bodyguards

Ages 24 & 26, Reno, Nevada. She/Her

The Death Heads are Music Man's rabid fan base who have traveled from all over to follow him. They have a cult-like reverence for the Music Man and listen to his every word. Most of the time they keep their distance from the rest of the raiders and prefer to set up their tent cities where they can party for days.

Starting Inventory: Fire Breathing Stick, Paintballs

Eat, Pray, Shove: DMG -5 When a Death Head attempts to commandeer a vehicle, they will use the handle of their fire breathing torch to assault the driver and try to shove them out of the driver seat. Driver must make an **Action Check +2** to resist or be shoved out of the vehicle.

Firestarter: DMG 0 After mastering the art of Fire Breathing at their favorite desert artist gathering, they're always glad to show off and get some practice in. This fire breathing attack can

15 LP
Action 6
Brains 5
Brawn 6
Cool 5
Charm 4
Guts 7

affect multiple vehicles in a 5-foot area and will continue to burn for three turns, doing an additional 5 LP damage each turn or until extinguished.

Namstayback: Instead of attacking, the Death Heads may spit fire into the air to make the Music Man's Escalade harder to target. While the flames are burning, the Music Man and his Escalade will get a -2 damage reduction on all attacks against them for the player's next turn.

Special Ability - Glow Stick: Instead of attacking, the Death Heads may hurl paintballs at an enemy or enemy vehicle that will result in a chemiluminescence response causing that player or vehicle to glow and become easier to target. Any glowing surface will take one additional LP damage per attack for three turns.

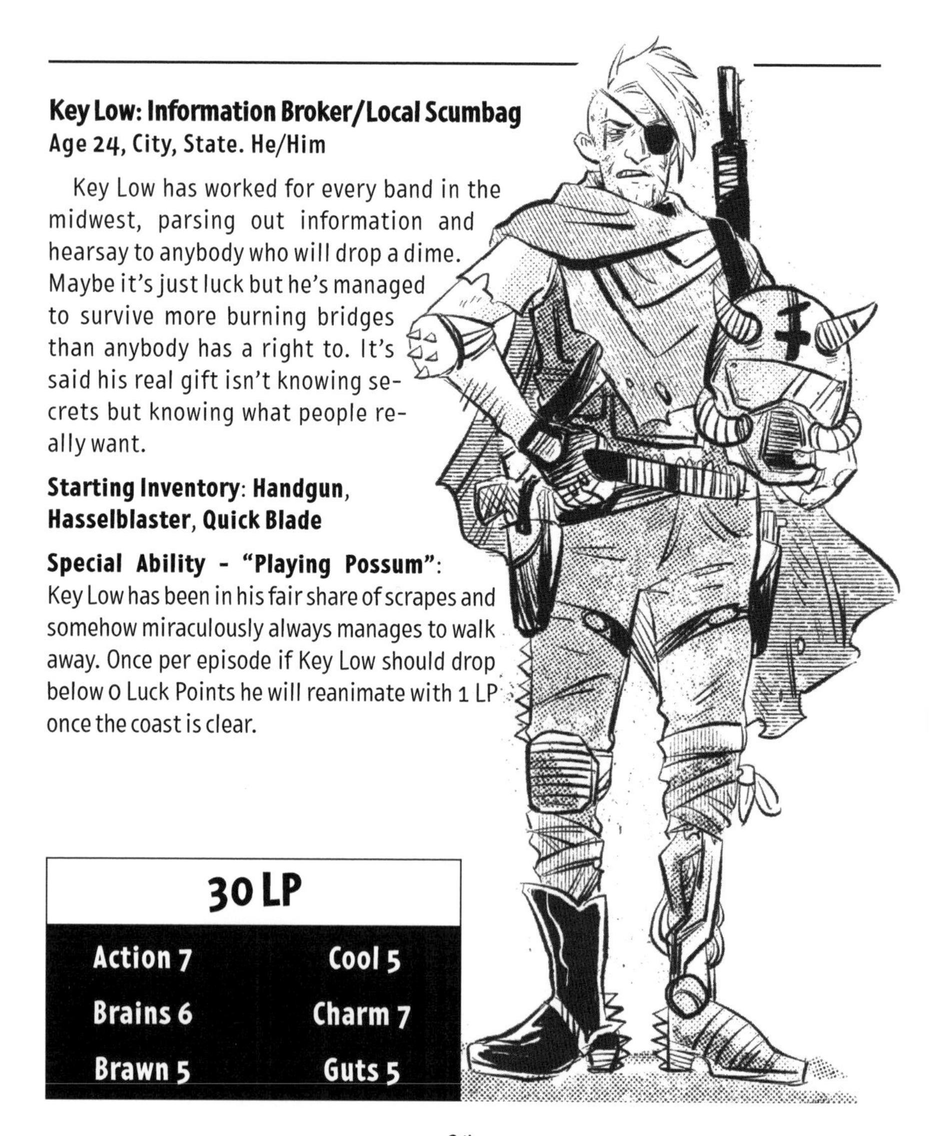

Key Low: Information Broker/Local Scumbag

Age 24, City, State. He/Him

Key Low has worked for every band in the midwest, parsing out information and hearsay to anybody who will drop a dime. Maybe it's just luck but he's managed to survive more burning bridges than anybody has a right to. It's said his real gift isn't knowing secrets but knowing what people really want.

Starting Inventory: **Handgun, Hasselblaster, Quick Blade**

Special Ability - "Playing Possum": Key Low has been in his fair share of scrapes and somehow miraculously always manages to walk away. Once per episode if Key Low should drop below 0 Luck Points he will reanimate with 1 LP once the coast is clear.

30 LP	
Action 7	Cool 5
Brains 6	Charm 7
Brawn 5	Guts 5

Scorp: Death Point Raider's Leader

Age 29, Parts Unknown. He/Him

Scorp is a brilliant tactician and strategist and he has spent the last few years building up his private army to overthrow what he views as corruption. He knows the key to accomplishing his mission isn't just brute force, although he has managed to create a modern formidable fighting force, but also the creation of myths and legends that can win a battle before a shot is ever fired.

Starting Inventory: Cigarettes, **Handgun**, Matches, **Quick Blade**

Special Ability: Empty The Bench : Not wanting to waste any more of his "Varsity" players, once per turn Scorp can call in 1d10 Dweebs on Mini Bikes as backup.

30 LP	
Action 7	Cool 3
Brains 5	Charm 4
Brawn 8	Guts 7

Naa Zaa: Death Point Raider's Second-In-Command

Age 25, Parts Unknown. He/Him

Legend of the Naa Zaa fills the cautionary bedtime stories of the midwest. Some speak of a man, or what used to be a man, riding a chopper covered in flames while others tell of a man so damaged by an explosion that he received a unique injection that made him immortal. Stories are all well and good, but the Naa Zaa's life is no fairy tale and he spends every day in terrible pain which causes him to hate every living thing.

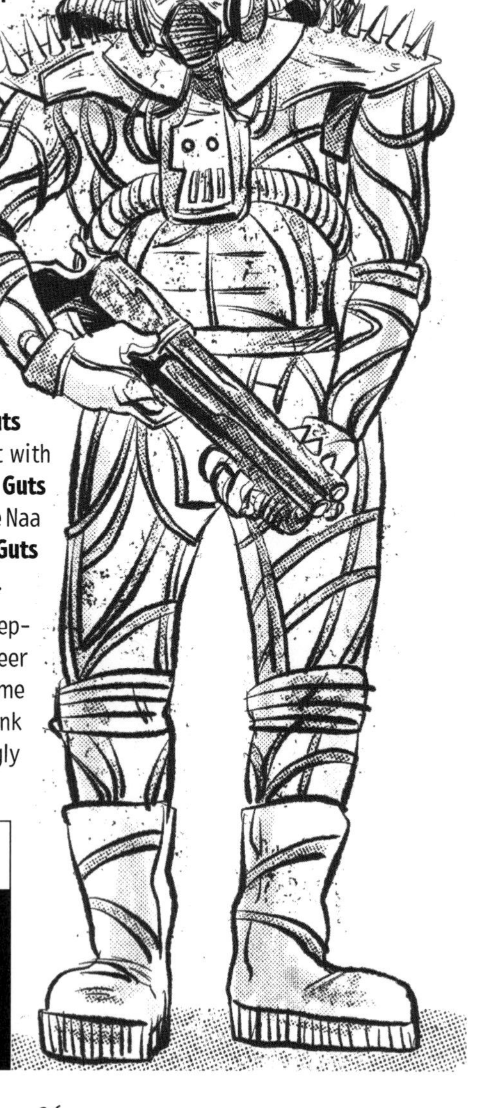

Starting Inventory: Hasselblaster Shotgun, Shock Baton

Special Ability - Ignite: Once per episode, the Naa Zaa may push the "Ignition" button on his jumpsuit resulting in his entire body becoming engulfed in flames for three turns. While engulfed, the Naa Zaa's Brawn increases to 9 and he will do DMG -5 to anything that his body comes in contact with. Should a player attempt to commandeer the Naa Zaa's vehicle they must make a **Guts Check +3** each turn they are in contact with the Naa Zaa's burning body or take a **Guts Penalty** in addition to damage. Once the Naa Zaa's flame dies down he will receive 3 **Guts Penalties** and all his stats will drop by 1.

Special Ability - Zero Gravity: Once per episode the Naa Zaa can jump to commandeer a vehicle with no Check by releasing some compressed air from his oxygen tank and floating through the air, seemingly weightless.

30 LP	
Action 7	Cool 3
Brains 5	Charm 4
Brawn 7	Guts 7

Blue Dragons

An ex-military pilot forced to retire because of his arthritis, Dudley's found employment flying old warbirds at air shows. As the midwest got stripped away and fell under corporate law, Dudley became more and more of a recluse hiding away at his ranch. The Blue Dragons began slowly with a few followers but quickly gained in numbers when word of their air superiority hit the streets. Typical Blue Dragons wear brown bomber jackets with the Blue Dragon logo and WW2 style leather helmets with goggles.

Dudley: Blue Dragon Squadron Leader

Age 55, Wichita, Kansas. He/Him

26 LP
Action 5
Brains 6
Brawn 4
Cool 4
Charm 3
Guts 7

Description: Dudley isn't so much a leader as a guy with a big house and badass plane. He keeps the Blue Dragons busy with chores and well fed with plenty of missions. He's always looking for any reason to take his plane to the sky.

Starting Inventory: US Air Force Challenge Coin, **Handgun**

Special Ability - Maverick: Dudley gained notoriety around the midwest air show circuit by performing airborne stunts only previously seen on the silver screen. Once per episode he may forgo an attack to take evasive maneuvers and receive a -5 damage reduction for Dragonheart on the player's next turn and a +3 damage bonus on his next attack.

Blue Dragon Soldier

Age 19-25, Wichita, Kansas. Any Pronouns

22 LP
Action 6
Brains 5
Brawn 6
Cool 5
Charm 4
Guts 5

Blue Dragon's Soldiers come from all walks of life but share a communal discomfort with the chaos the apocalypse wrought. Having a daily structure and orders to follow gave them a new purpose in the wasteland and a found family. Unconcerned with rank, they are content in their equality, only looking to Dudley for leadership and direction.

Starting Inventory: **Handgun**, **Rifle** or **Sub Machine Gun**

Special Ability - Hold The Line: Once per episode, when two or more Blue Devils form up and attack in unison, they will each gain a damage bonus of +1. Any Blue Devil attacking or being attacked at range behind them will receive a damage reduction of a -3.

Slaughter Sisters

The Slaughter Sisters are one of the more extreme bands out on the plains. They were founded by Borgir, who never felt they belonged anywhere but found a modicum of celebrity in gladiatorial combat at the Arena. She picked two Lieutenants, TUuala and Azraph, to help them demonstrate midwest justice.

Borgir: Slaughter Sisters Leader

Age 23, Pacific, Missouri. They/Them

Borgir found themselves after they dismissed all notions of being weak. The way to survive is by being strong, and they are the strongest leader with the strongest band driving the strongest vehicles. That's how they rose to be undefeated in the Resolv Center.

Starting Inventory: Hasselblaster Shotgun

Special Ability - Bathory's Blood Bath: Borgir relishes in the pain of others and is no stranger to going to great lengths to show their commitment to carnage. Once per episode, Borgir may cover themself in the blood of their enemies and regain 5 Luck Points.

26 LP	
Action 5	Cool 4
Brains 6	Charm 3
Brawn 4	Guts 7

TUuala: Slaughter Sister Lieutenant

Age 19, Pacific, Missouri. She/Her

22 LP
Action 5
Brains 6
Brawn 4
Cool 4
Charm 3
Guts 7

TUala's father sold her and her mother off to cover gambling debts, forcing them into a life of abuse and grueling work. Her mother coped with it by becoming incredibly devout in her religion. TUuala grew frustrated by her mother wishing life would become better and never doing anything about it. The sudden and tragic death of her mother from pneumonia left her distraught and lost. TUuala was at her wit's end when she decided to try the prayer her mother had so fervently believed in. She didn't know any traditional psalms so she recited a verse of "Raining Blood" instead. Moments later Borgir entered her life like an avenging angel of death.

Starting Inventory: Hasselblaster Shotgun

Special Ability - Knights In Satan's Service: TUula's faith comes from the Gods of Metal and she acts as their Unholy Paladin through that faith. Once per episode, TUula may steel herself and invoke her Dark Lord, The Holy Diver, granting her a -5 reduction to damage for one turn.

Azraph: Slaughter Sisters Weaponmaster

Age 18, Pacific, Missouri. She/Her

23 LP	
Action 5	Cool 4
Brains 6	Charm 3
Brawn 4	Guts 7

Azraph worked for the Black Swans as a heavy weaponsmith. On a day off she went to the Resolv Center and saw the Slaughter Sisters destroy a minor Band. Starstruck by the bloodlust and wanton violence she had witnessed she requested leave to join the Slaughter Sisters. Since the Slaughter Sister's dole out justice for the Black Swans anyway the leave was happily granted. Azraph upgraded Borgir's truck with the Gore Gun and was made an official Slaughter Sister on the spot.

Starting Inventory: Hasselblaster Shotgun

Special Ability - I Love It When A Plan Comes Together: When she was younger, Azraph stayed with her uncle, an army vet who had a sick DVD collection. She spent long afternoons watching reruns of the A-Team and MacGuyver, mystified by how they could make weapons out of literally anything they found lying around. Inspired by this, she can make a weapon out of almost anything. Once per episode, Azraph may forgo an attack to build a single-use makeshift weapon DMG +2.

The Urchins existed in the slums of the city, doing their best to scrape by. Joe Disorder was the loudest and most obnoxious so naturally he was elected leader. They are generally younger than most other bands but exemplify the time honored tradition of juvenile delinquents wearing t-shirts, jeans, denim jackets, and spiky hair.

Joe Disorder: Urchin Leader

Age 14. Arkansas City, Kansas He/Him

19 LP
Action 6
Brains 4
Brawn 6
Cool 3
Charm 3
Guts 4

Some babies are born kicking and screaming, and some never stop. That's Joe Disorder.

Starting Inventory: Potato Gun Cannon, Punk'in Bombs, Slingshot, Quick Blade

Slingshot: MV 5ft, 5 M80s, DMG -2

Punk'in Bombs: 5 Bombs, DMG +3 Joe Disorder's' "Punk'in Bombs" are nothing more than a handful of M80s duct taped around a box of nails and spray painted orange. They will do max damage to their intended target and half damage to anything within a 10-foot radius, including Joe Disorder, should he be unable to flee.

Special Ability - Snot Rocket: 6 Globs, DMG -6 The Urchin's created a compressed air-powered Potato Gun Cannon that they've mounted to the Copter that launches sticky electrically charged globs of acidic slime at its enemies. Upon impact, these globs will adhere to their target, disrupting its electrical current and thus decreasing its overall performance and ability.

Special Ability - Cut and Run: If Joe Disorder is on foot or in a vehicle that a player is attempting to commandeer he will cut a fart so nasty that the player must make a **Guts Check** to keep their bearings. They cannot attack him if they fail, and he may escape. If Joe does the commandeering, he will have a -2 to **Brawn Checks** to push the driver out of the vehicle.

GR Notes: This special ability will not work in open-air vehicles

---

Steet Punx: Urchin Soldier

Ages 12-14, Any Pronouns

24 LP
Action 5
Brains 6
Brawn 4
Cool 4
Charm 3
Guts 7

They aren't old enough to drink, drive, smoke, vote, or die on the front lines but that won't stop them from boosting your car and joy riding through the city.

Starting Inventory: Handgun, Molotov Cocktail

Special Ability - Squatter's Rights: Even before the war the Street Punx had become accustomed to people trying to eject them from the places they claimed for themself. With this in mind, they developed strategies to dig their heels into their occupancy. The Punx may forgo an attack to gain a -3 damage reduction on their enemies' next turn and a +1 damage bonus to their next attack.

HEXIES

Living in the hills, the Hexies Coven has created a near-mythical status. Tales of curses, magic, and being taken in the night have most kids wishing they never come face to face with the Hexies. The mere sound of ripper ATVs saws in the night makes most want to run. The rumors are a shield; the truth is they live in a relatively peaceful coven-based matriarchy.

Red Wolfe: Hexie's Leader

Age 29. She/Her

24 LP
Action 5
Brains 6
Brawn 4
Cool 4
Charm 3
Guts

The third leader of the Coven. An ex-marine, she has trained the Coven to be an elite hit-and-run squad, allowing them to take what they need and disappear into rumors.

Starting Inventory: Handgun, Hasselblaster, Smoke Bombs, Quick Blade

Special Ability - The Howling: Once per episode, Red Wolfe may forgo an attack and bray into the sky, granting all the Hexies a -1 bonus to their **Action Checks** and a +1 bonus to their damage rolls for one turn. On her next turn, Red Wolf will gain a +2 damage bonus on her first attack.

Hexie Wildling: Hexie Soldier 20 LP

Ages 12-20, Any Pronouns

20 LP
Action 5
Brains 6
Brawn 4
Cool 4
Charm 3
Guts

Made up of women from all walks of life, the Hexie Coven is the post-apocalyptic remanifestation of the ancient Amazons. They follow their leaders fearlessly and obey their bylaws fervently.

Special Ability - The Mist: The Hexies may forgo an attack to set off multiple Smoke Bombs on the battlefield, obscuring the vision of both air and ground vehicles while granting themselves a -2 damage reduction and a plus +2 damage bonus on all their attacks.

Smoke Bombs: Perry Party Compay's Rainbow Bombs were all the rage at outdoor summer festivals back in 2031. These multi-colored bombs were easy to sneak in due to their diminutive size (about the size of a large brussels sprout) and easy to use because they could be set off by striking the fuse against almost any surface. After finding a surplus in a local party store on a raid, the Hexies use them to add to their mayhem and mystique.

BLACK SWANS

The Black Swans are not a band in the traditional sense. They may have begun as one but now they mostly police other bands and "keep the peace" in the wasteland. Led by Mrs. Olivia and funded by Resolv Corp, the Black Swans maintain order by overwhelming force and by pitting bands against one another. They use extortion, misinformation, and when all else fails, the Resolv Corp center where grudges are made into a spectacle for an audience.

Mrs. Olivia: Black Swan Leader

Age 27. Lowell, Massachusetts She/Her

30 LP
Action 7
Brains 6
Brawn 6
Cool 3
Charm 3
Guts 6

In the Amphikura war, Mrs. Olivia's clandestine tactical units were codenamed Black Swans. They ran successful mission after mission for the military, but she couldn't help feeling like Sisyphus. Every battle won meant two more losses to the Amphkura. That's when Resolv Corp approached her to be a private contractor with the promise of unlimited resources. She just had to maintain peace and stop the country's collapse. Once she achieved that, she could refocus their efforts back to the front. She expanded upon the Black Swans by recruiting the best and molding them into a powerful force. Resolv kept moving the goalposts on their agreement, burdening her with more and more administrative work and removing her from the frontlines entirely. She eventually lost touch with how bad things had gotten.

Starting Inventory: Handgun, Nightrider

Nightrider MV 0ft, 10 Round Magazine, DMG -1 See pg 51 for stats.

Special Ability - "I'm Not Even Supposed To Be Here Today": Once per episode Mrs. Olivia may forgo an attack to instead call in reinforcements and add 1d10 Black Swan Soldiers to the battlefield acting as ground troops. On a roll of 10, the troops will begrudgingly show up but only do half damage on all attacks as they will be "phoning it in" for the combat.

Black Swan Soldier: General Enlisted

Ages 18-27, Any Pronouns

A private army that masquerades as a "band" from the wasteland to maintain order.

Starting Inventory: Handgun, Sniper Rifle, Submachine Gun

Special Ability - Human Shield: Once per episode, a Black Swan soldier may forgo their attack to absorb half the damage that would have been done to Mrs. Oliva on the player's next turn by operating as her "human shield", effectively shielding her from damage.

24 LP
Action 7
Brains 5
Brawn 6
Cool 4
Charm 3
Guts 7

Weapons

Avery SW-85 Sub Machine Gun

MV 30ft, 20 Round Magazine, DMG -3

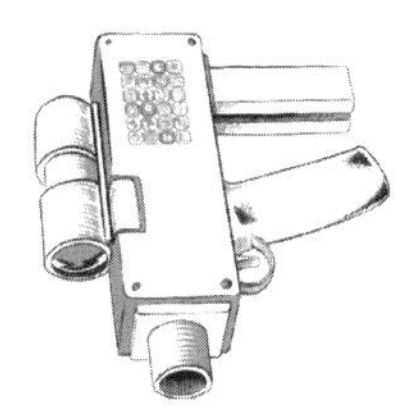

This lightweight semi-automatic was pioneered by the CIA and Avery Firearms as a compact smart device and offensive weapon. Made from 80% recycled materials, the SW-85 is great for stealthier missions where it is necessary to travel light and tight but still stay in touch with HQ.

Special Ability - She's Automatic: The Hellsings converted this semi-automatic pistol to full automatic in an attempt to quickly waste the other gangs while driving. When the trigger is pulled the bullets won't stop flying until released. So if you choose to, you may unload the full magazine in one shot. DMG -7

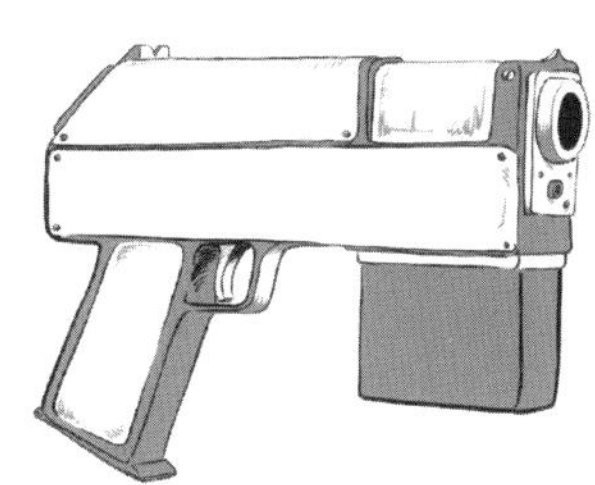

Avery JP-77 Handgun

MV 30ft, 15 Round Magazine, DMG -3

The JP-77 Handgun was the preferred handgun of midwestern law enforcement professionals from 2037 to the current day. It was so prevalent that their manufacturer, Avery Firearms, once bragged they had moved 5 million units within the first three years.

Special ABility - Disarm: Can be used to disarm an enemy with a weapon. To disarm, target the weapon and then make a damage roll. As long as the damage is done, any standard weapon will be destroyed. It can also trigger environmental effects like breaking chains, severing ropes, triggering traps, or exploding a flame thrower.

Wilcox H-50 "Hasselblaster 777" Triple Barrel Shotgun

MV 20ft, 6 Round Barrel, DMG -1

After legislation was passed in the fall of 2032 to severely curtail the sale of semi-automatic weapons to the general public a void was created in the recreational gun sales market. Wilcox Firearms saw the need for something with a little more stopping power and had the Hasselblaster 777 on shelves the following spring. Its designer, Sam Morgan, named it after his old drinking buddy Mark, who was by all accounts a real swell guy.

Special Ability - This Is My Boom Stick: When firing at point-blank range, the damage bonus increases to +3. If you don't kill your opponent outright, they will immediately perform a counterattack.

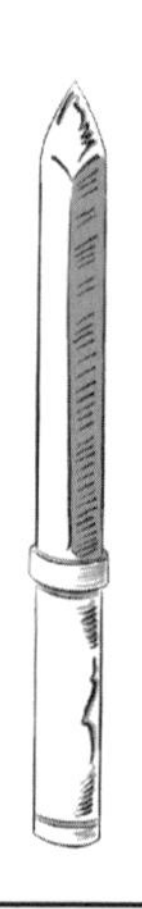

Van Zandt Quick Blade (Knife)
MV 40ft, DMG -4

The Van Zandt Technologies Quick Blade came into vogue in 2030 when the military sought new (more cost-effective) lighter alternatives to many of their standard weapons. Touted as being lighter, sharper, and perfectly balanced, the US military found the Quick Blade to be just as advertised. By 2031 they were the standard blade carried by all soldiers across all branches of the military.

Special Ability - Sneak Attack: A successful **Action Check** to sneak means you can make a Stealth Attack and the DMG penalty drops to 0. If you don't kill your enemy outright, they get to attack with a damage penalty of 0.

Van Zandt Shock Baton
MV 40ft, DMG -4

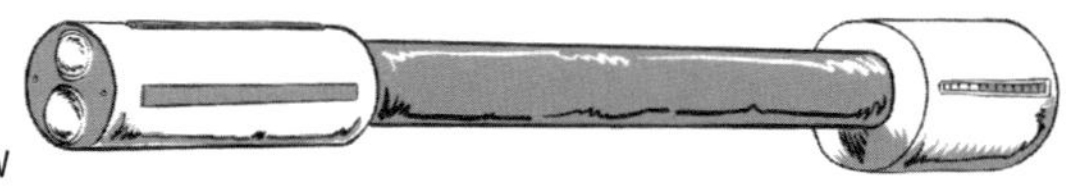

Initially designed as a new style of solar-powered cattle prod, the Shock Baton was adopted by law enforcement and repurposed as a way for riot police to keep protesters in line during the early days of the apocalypse. After they eventually abandoned their posts, a surplus of Shock Batons were lying around and thus they became a common weapon on the streets.

Special Ability - Danger! High Voltage: After making a successful **Action Check** to board an enemy combatant's vehicle, the player may use this special ability to stun the driver of the vehicle, forcing them to make a **Brawn Check +3** or be launched from the vehicle and freeing up the driver seat for the player.

Magnet Hatchets
MV 5ft, DMG -5

Paul Ox, a small-time inventor, had a big idea one drunken winter night in 2027 at the House of Axe in Duluth, Minnesota. As he tired of walking the 15 feet to the target to regain his hatchet he thought, "what if they came back?". So Paul spent the rest of the winter refining his idea and the Magnet Hatchets were born (with sixteen prototypes and two lost fingers later)! These twin steel hatchets can be thrown and then called back to their owner's hand by a magnetic sensor in a glove.

Special Ability - Stuck On You: When attempting to board an enemy vehicle or climb onto a higher surface, the Hatchets will grant their owner a -2 bonus to **Action Checks**.

Captain Hook's Bowling Bombs

MV 0ft, DMG -1

Many great amateur bomb makers came and went during the early days of the apocalypse, but none of them had even an ounce of the panache Rusty "Captain" Hook did. He made a small fortune by marrying the supplies he had left over from his fireworks shop and the bowling balls from the Bowling Alley he was shacked up in. Each ball is filled with M80s and can be rolled at enemy vehicles or dropped from above with explosive results. People still talk about how ol' Rusty picked up that last spare, saving some kids from the Black Swans out by the old Eastwood Bridge.

Special Ability - Gutterball: Will create a Pot Hole if exploded on asphalt resulting in a +2 penalty to **Action Checks** for the enemy driver.

Wilcox E-34 "Eagle Eye" Sniper Rifle

MV 0ft, 10 Round Magazine, DMG -1

2033 was a very profitable year for Wilcox as they followed up the windfall from the Hasselblaster in Q2 with the release of their Eagle Eye Sniper Rifle in Q3, just before the holiday season. This lightweight rifle, also designed by Sam Morgan, was close enough to military grade without being under a government contract.

Special Ability - Long Distance Call: Can target enemies several maps ahead. A miss might trigger an attack of all nearby enemies.

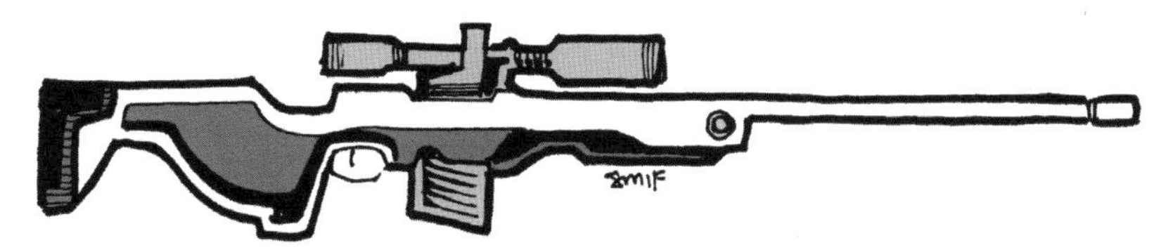

Molotov Cocktail

MV 5ft, 1 Bottle, DMG +3

Probably stolen from somebody's suburban dad's liquor cabinet, this 151 Proof homemade incendiary device is exactly what every young pyromaniac needs to commit their first arson. For those living on the outskirts, the same could be achieved with a mason jar, a dirty rag, and two pints of Sluiceshine. Although, for the record, Sluiceshine goes down a lot smoother than 151, so always use the rum first.

Burning Down The House: Once exploded, if the cocktail is not extinguished after the initial ignition, the flames will continue to grow. The surface impacted will receive half damage and one **Guts Penalty** each turn until the fire is put out or the target is wasted.

Specail Ability - Firestarter: Instead of being thrown, the Molotov Cocktail may be poured out onto the street and lit up, causing a Road Hazard.

Wilcox AS-92 Grenade Launcher

MV 5ft, 6 Round Bandolier, DMG Explosive Rounds +4, Smoke Round, Illumination Round.

This lightweight armament is the first weapon of its kind to weigh less than 3lbs, giving the US infantry a little extra muscle during the early days of the war. The AS-92's design was a well guarded and proprietary secret until one day in the summer of 2029 a hacker named "**MLTDPOPSIKL**" gained access into a local military server, downloading and sharing the schematics. The good news is that bands could now 3D print Grenade Launchers. The bad news is that it was MLTDPOPSIKL's last transmission.

Special Ability - Boom: Explosive rounds will cause mass damage but must be fired at a distance as it will affect anything in range upon detonation.

Special Ability - Befuddle: Smoke rounds obscure vision in a 20 ft sphere. Ranged attacks through the smoke get a -3 to damage.

Special Ability - Bright: Illumination rounds set off a phosphorous flare that can be visible up to a mile away. Will combust any dry materials it is around.

Miscellaneous Weapons

Bowling Pins: DMG -7

Chains: DMG -6

Crowbar: DMG -5

Hockey Stick: DMG -6

Paint Can: DMG -6

Trash Can: DMG -9

Special Weapons

Wilcox K-82 Nightrider

MV 0ft, 10 Round Magazine, DMG -1

In 2035 the US government commissioned Wilcox to create what would be considered the "next big thing" in modern warfare; the Nightrider. This extremely lightweight, long-range sniper rifle is made up of 90% recycled materials and balanced to the point that even a civilian could easily hit a bullseye from 50 yards. In the hands of a trained sniper, however, the Nightrider becomes a two-mile extension of Death's boney touch.

The Nightrider boasts perfect balance and has a reflectionless scope that offers perfect sight day, night, or when using infrared to pick up heat signatures. This, coupled with a built-in self-repairing silencer, makes the Nightrider every sniper's dream and a nightmare for every unknowing victim.

Special Ability - Lights Out: Unlike other weapons that may only attack the vehicle, the Nightrider can be used to attack the rider of any vehicle they can see or spot through their scope directly. The shot may be taken from a distance of up to 2 miles, and should the assailant decide to perform their assault from a closer range the built-in silencer will prevent their position from being given away.

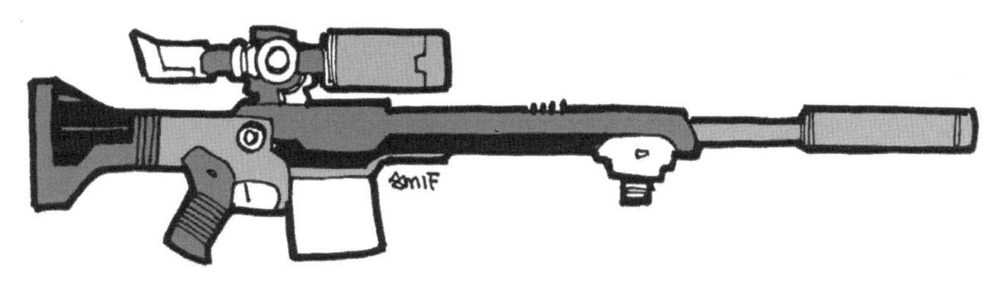

Van Zandt "Black Cat" Grappling Gun

MV 40ft, DMG -7 (-1 bonus to Action Checks when commandeering a vehicle).

The US military was so impressed by the Quick Blade that they ordered the Van Zandt "Black Cat" Grapple Gun sight unseen. Based on a 2007 design sold to the company by an anonymous scientist, the current version is lighter, more compact, and can be wielded with one hand. While still used by the military to this day, the Black Cat is the preferred fashion accessory to wasteland car thieves.

Special Ability - "Where Do You Think You're Going?": DMG -8 Can be used offensively to pierce and pull a distant opponent in for an attack at DMG 0. If you don't kill your enemy outright, they will immediately make a counterattack with a damage penalty of 0, and you will not be able to use the Grappling Gun again until your opponent is dead.

CHILDREN OF UMA

Player's Preface

50 years after the sun cooked the Earth's ass, life is surprisingly the same. Too many mouths, too few spoons. Only thing different is people ain't as polite as they used to be. Being polite gets you taken out and not even necessarily by another band, just the Earth itself doesn't respect politeness anymore. So you fight for your band and they fight for you. Whatever it takes. But with a little Carbon + and a dream, you can make your way. That said, it ain't ever gonna be easy.

Croc

Leader of the Hellsings

The apocalypse wasn't an event so much as a slow crawl into a new reality that resembled prehistoric times. The dawn of a Neo Dark Age. The convenience of a big city became a death trap. People manage on the fringe in groups, called bands, trying to survive. Each band has its own goals, some big and some small. Yours is small.

The Hellsings.

The Hellsings were founded by Croc.

Croc used to be a member of a bigger band, The Black Swans, but he had a disagreement and left them with a few less heads. Also might have lifted a few items too. They tried to hunt him down but he's got a preternatural resistance to death.

Why is he called Croc? He got that name from his leathery skin. You see, Croc is a child of UMA. What's UMA? It's just one of humanity's many mistakes. Oh, there were so many mistakes leading up to the end of all things. UMA was a mutagen that originated somewhere in space and landed deep in the ocean. It should have stayed there submerged forever, but the world's governments kept playing around until they refined it into something else. *If you wanna learn more about the origins of UMA check out Rocket to Russia and Point Nemo. But it ain't necessary for this adventure*

Croc is a savvy killer. He's whip-smart, likes to watch and observe, then explode.

You feel under Croc you might have a chance.

Episode 1: In Through the Out Door

GR notes: Like most Post Apocalyptic movies or games, **Children of UMA** begins with a narrator setting the tone for the new world the audience will be in for a little while. The following is a speech Croc gives the players to get psyched for the upcoming raid.

"Our clan is small. Real small, about 20 heads. But you are all mad as hell. Crazier than a squad of bots. The Hellsings are makin' a reputation. They say the world is fixin' itself, but who wants to wait 150 million years. We need to live now," Croc says.

"Keylow is a scumbag information broker who said a Death Point Raiders caravan would be riding up past the ash fields. Keylow said they were gonna be carrying guns, drugs, and fun. He also said lots of Raiders got wasted last quarter moon so we should be park walking. They are looking to relocate their operation. Scorp put his number 1, the Naa Zaa, in charge of this one. Should be light and tight."

"First, take out the rear guard. They are down on rides so you need to blow the mobile barracks. That will take out a bunch of soldiers. Cap the Music Man next. That should sow some chaos and disarray. After that, take out the Naa Zaa. You'll be cutting off Scorps' right hand. Then we'll run the plains."

You know that look in Croc's eyes. That's the look that took you from the gravel into the hills. Nobody messes with Croc. Everybody listens 'cause he's "the man with the plan".

"Now listen, I don't trust Keylow, so keep your eyes peeled for trouble. At 6 am you ride and you take what's theirs!"

GR Notes: After this speech it's a good time to check on your players and make sure everybody is okay. It's also a good time to discuss any misunderstanding of rules or characters. Once gameplay begins you will be doing the scenes back to back and it should take about an hour and a half to two hours to complete the module.

Scene 1: Back Of The Bus With The Cool Kids

The wall of silt and dirt is about a mile high and to the east today. A blanket of filth that rises straight to the sky and blots the sun so that it looks like a distant pearl centered in a suffocating quilt of pink and purple— blanketing the 30-mile stretch of broken highway. On a positive note, the pink and purple look nice.

Croc scoped out a small abandoned red barn in a fallow cornfield. That's where you are going to spring your trap.

Bass is the first thing you hear, shaking the earth like a thousand hooves, relentless in time, and growing louder with each beat. It's followed by the rumble, the lighting crash to the thunder shaking the planet.

The convoy bursts onto the scene, erupting past your cover and exploding up the highway at full speed. It's long, a lot longer than you thought. A voice in your head says this might not be the best idea as you watch the cars plow forward.

Croc comes in over your helmet radio and says, "It's time!".

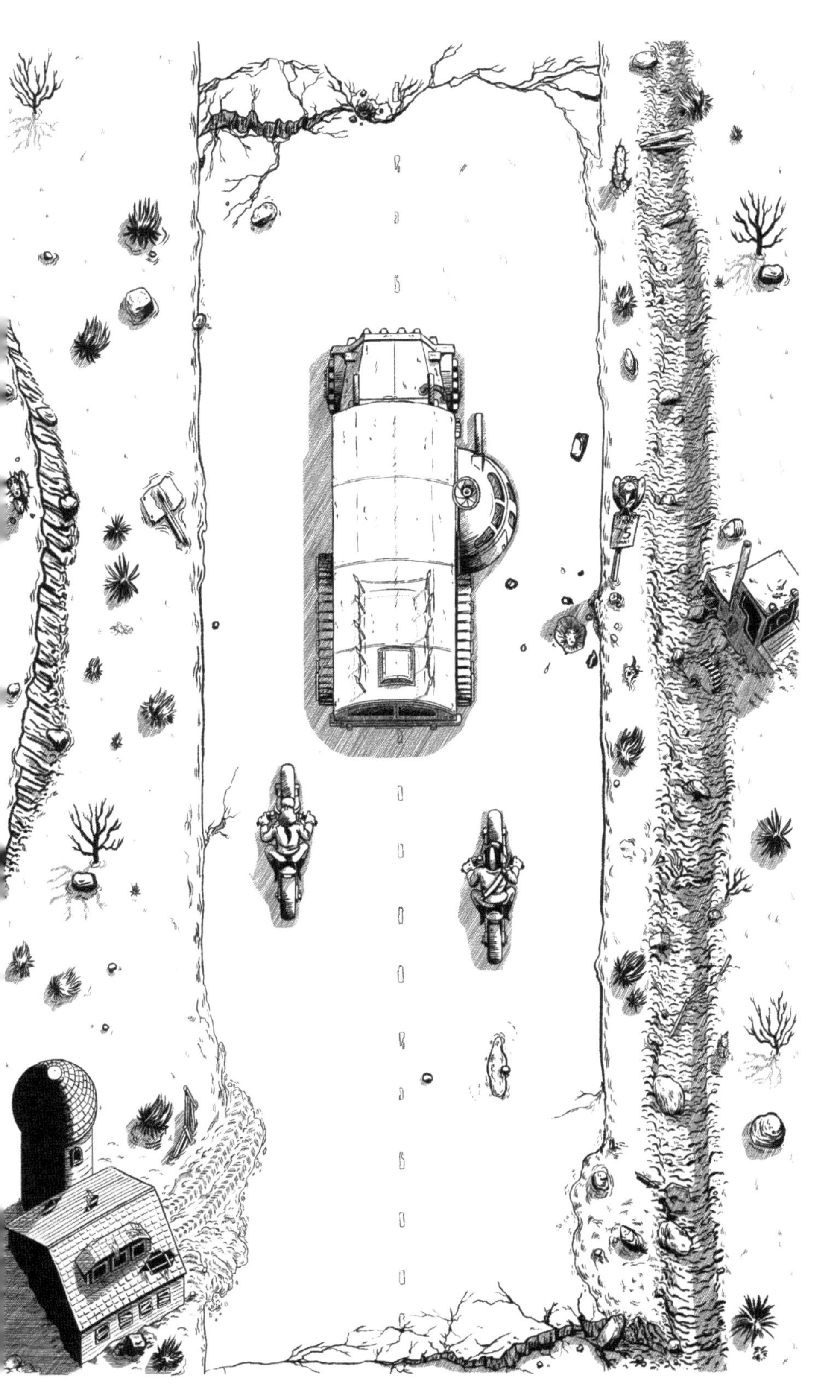
75

As the players pull onto the highway and head into combat they will be making their approach at the tail end of the convoy. The rear guard consists of **Two Motorcycle Dweebs** on bikes and it should be easy combat, just challenging enough to allow the players and GR a brief encounter to get the first battle out of the way. If your players are a little more experienced, you can include the **School Bus** in the first encounter.

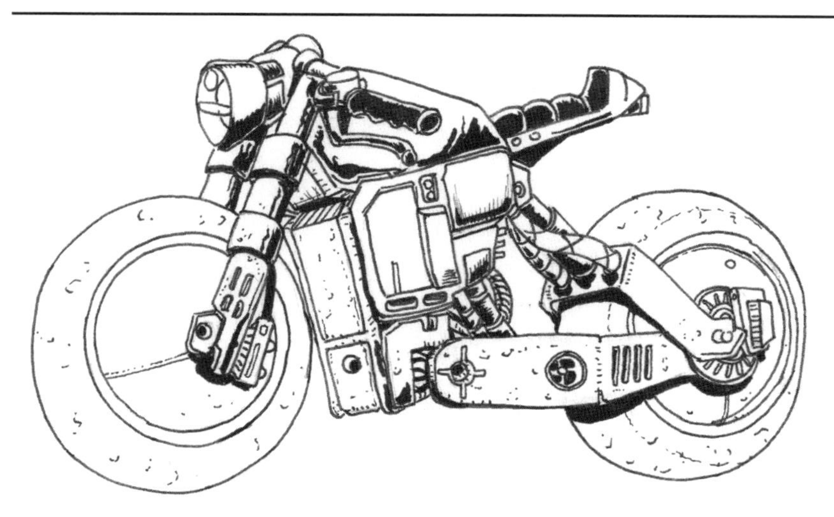

Dweebs Motorcycles

7ft Length, 2ft Width, 2ft Height, 480lbs., One Rider

15 LP
Action 8
Brains
Brawn 3
Cool
Charm
Guts 4

Description: This "Cafe Racer" style motorcycle was made famous by Jonny Reves in the classic crime thriller Out For Revenge. It is also the one where most recently divorced fathers would be seen riding around Kansas City in the mid to late 2040s.

1 Attack + 1 SA Per Turn

Kick/Punch: MV 5ft DMG -6

Unchained: DMG -4 The "Motorcycle Dweebs" come wrapped in leather and 6 feet of heavy steel chains and when they are in striking distance of an enemy vehicle they will unfurl their chains and slash and whip their foes with them. Should their chain attack yield no damage, the chain smacks into their own bike and will be ripped from their hand, resulting in 2 LP damage.

Special Ability - Hard to Kill: While weaving in and out of traffic, the rider can get one attack on another vehicle from any direction. Using this SA will also grant them a -1 Luck Point damage reduction on their next turn, as they will be harder to hit while performing this ability.

GR Notes: Since this is the first combat, we recommend a straight bit of highway with no Road Hazards to allow the players to become comfortable with vehicular combat.

Combat Stage 1: Once the Dweebs are attacked they will fire back at their opponents with their Sub Machine Guns and attempt to keep a distance between the players and the convoy. They will fully engage on their second turn.

After the Dweebs are taken care of the player can progress to the next part of the convoy.

Read the following:

> The green and black school bus swerves and writhes like an insect, teeming with arms and legs reaching through each window and opening.
>
> The back door of the bus swings open and two Dweebs on minibikes jettison out while swinging chains above their heads. Another Dweeb jumps into a passenger-side mounted turret while a hatch opens on the roof and two Dweebs with rifles position themselves. Meanwhile, a line of Dweebs starts throwing whatever garbage they can out the back doors.
>
> This school bus is battle-ready.

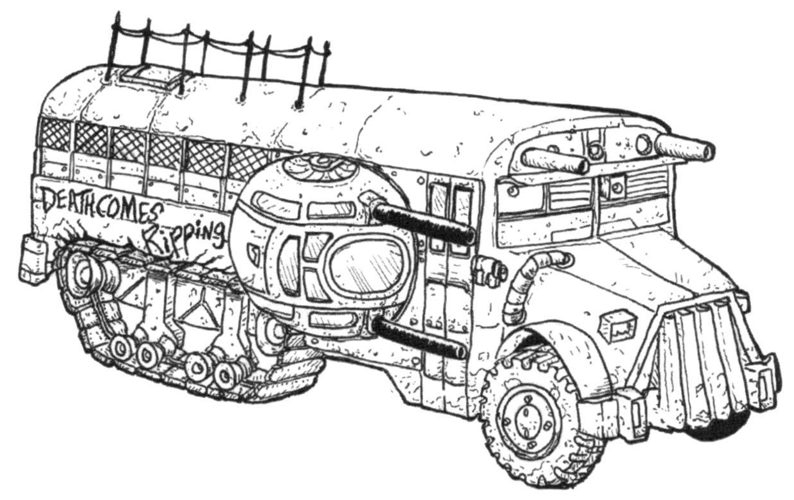

School Bus

45ft Length, 8ft Width, 11ft Height, 25,000 lbs., 15 Riders

Description: This early 2037 Traveler model schoolbus was the last in production before its maker, Rölf, shifted its business model to assist with the war effort. In its initial form the Traveler could seat up to 54 passengers plus the driver. However, in its current state, having made room for the Gun Turret, Mini Bikes, and weapons, it only seats 15.

1 Attack + 1 SA Per Turn

Passenger Side Turret: DMG 0 This heavily armored turret protects the School Bus from being passed on the right by its enemies, only dropping its guard to give its teammates access to the bus's side door.

50 LP

Action 5
Brains
Brawn 8
Cool
Charm
Guts 6

Back Of The Bus With The Cool Kids: Once the Mini Bike Dweebs have hit the road the rest of the Dweebs can throw garbage at their enemies. The damage varies by the type of items thrown.

Standing On A Rooftop Screaming: The Muscle Dweebs will access the bus's roof through the top emergency hatch at the back and either fire their weapons at their enemies or use the grappling gun to create a zip line to try and board and commandeer their vehicles. **Grappling Gun**: DMG -6

Special Ability - 5 Points On Your License: DMG +3 The school bus's left side is completely covered in sharp metal spikes. Any opponent that attempts to pass on the left will be slammed into and crushed against the side of the bus resulting in damage plus 1 **Guts Penalty**. Anything motorcycle-sized or smaller will immediately get dragged under the bus and destroyed.

GR Notes: One Dweeb will always be in the driver's seat, and one will stay in the pod for the entire encounter. After the two Dweebs on Mini Bikes hit the road, one Dweeb should be operating the back door throwing garbage while the remaining ten remain ready to hit the roof as needed.

Combat Stage 2: On the first turn of combat, the back emergency door of the Bus will pop open and two Dweebs on mini bikes will launch out the back onto the street and attack the nearest vehicle with chains.

Two Muscle Dweebs with rifles will climb on the roof and target air support vehicles. If there are no air support vehicles they will start to blast the smaller ground vehicles before moving on to larger vehicles.

The Turret Dweeb will shoot the largest ground vehicle in sight first before targeting and attacking the air support.

The road will remain straight and hazard-free.

Dweebs Mini Bike

5ft Length, 1.5ft Width, 2ft Height, 134lbs., One Ride

Description: These "fun sized" bikes were the top seller for a local motorcycle manufacturer, Bishop Motorsports, from 2032-2036. They were banned statewide by the Department of Education after some local dirtbags tore up the football field at Wichita High on the night before the state championship.

10 LP
Action 6
Brains
Brawn 3
Cool
Charm
Guts 3

1 Attack + 1 SA Per Turn

Kick/Punch: MV 5ft DMG -6

Molotov Cocktail: One Bottle, DMG +2 Each Mini Bike Dweeb comes with one Molotov Cocktail that they can use against their foe's vehicles. Once ignited, the flame will result in 1 **Guts Penalty** and continue to burn until extinguished or for the next two turns at -6 damage.

Special Ability - Hard to Kill: While weaving in and out of traffic the rider can get one attack on another vehicle from any direction. Using this SA will also grant them a -1 Luck Point damage reduction on their next turn as they will be harder to hit while performing this ability.

Special Ability - Sneak King: DMG + 3 Mini Bikes with an average-sized rider can move directly under some large-sized vehicles such as Semi Trucks doing damage directly to brake lines and other important equipment.

Combat Stage 3: On the second combat turn, the Bus will swerve right and then left, revealing two wrecked cars on the right side of the road and then a third a hundred feet up on the left before the road straightens out again. All vehicles except for the Bus must make an **Action Check +2** to avoid crashing into the wreckage. Any vehicle that fails will take 5 LP damage and 1 **Guts Penalty**.

The two Muscle Dweebs with rifles will continue to target air support vehicles. If there are no air support vehicles they will start to blast the smaller ground vehicles before moving on to larger vehicles.

The **Turret Dweeb** will shoot at whatever the highest perceived threat is.

Combat Stage 4 And Beyond: On the third combat turn, should the garbage Dweebs or Rifle Dweebs be killed, two more will take their place and continue the onslaught. This reinforcement will end either when the Bus is commandeered or destroyed or all fifteen Dweebs on board are dead.

GR notes: By the start of turn two, eight Dweebs will be in action (Driver, Garbage (2), Mini-Bike (2), Rooftop (2), and Turret Dweeb, which will shoot at whatever the highest perceived threat is). This leaves seven remaining Dweebs in support to do with as needed.

The players may progress to the next part of the convoy after the Bus has been dealt with.

Read the following:

Scene 2: No Requests

Music Man watches the chase in disgust. He spits a vile black liquid into a red solo cup then grabs the current record on his deck, making a massive scratch sound over the speakers. He breaks the vinyl over his knee before grabbing the mic.

"You want some fight music! Well, let me see those hands reach for the sky!"

He drops the needle and blaring music fills the air. You can feel the relentless kick drum pushing the tempo and you swear the purple clouds low on the horizon begins to pulse to the beat.

Music Man hits a button and steam shoots out the side of his Escalade. When it clears, a crazy-looking spiked truck appears flanked by ATVs.

"La Grange" Mobile Stage/SUV

17ft Length, 7ft Width, 8ft Height 6,000 lbs., One Rider

Description: Even before the war, the Music Man's SUV's (lovingly called "La Grange") was customized within an inch of its life to become "The Midwest's Ultimate Mobile Party stage"!. It was recently upgraded using US military technology meant to battle the Amphikura. The Music Man's SUV has a cutting-edge sonic arsenal that also doubles as the Music Man's current DJ Rig since he has severe hearing damage from years spent on the club circuit without ear protection.

1 Attack + 1 SA Per Turn

On The 1's And 2's: DMG -4 The Music Man's stage will spin around and while he rips it up on the turntables four buzzsaw blades will shoot out of his DJ booth tearing into any vehicle riding behind his Escalade, friend and foe alike.

Special Ability - Foam Party: The Music Man's Escalade blows nonflammable foam from its tailpipe that will expand and cover the road causing all in its path a -2 penalty to **Action Checks** while granting the Escalade a -1 damage reduction for the next two turns.

Special Ability - The Drop: DMG -5 The Music Man will turn his stage towards his opponents and build the beat up to a crescendo before hitting them with the Drop. This sonic boom attack will hit all vehicles in its path, resulting in damage and 1 **Guts Penalty**.

35 LP
Action 6
Brains
Brawn 8
Cool
Charm
Guts 8

Combat Stage 1: Flanking the Music Man are two women riding ATVs and they are high as hell. Once the bus is defeated, they peel from the entourage position and race towards the Hellsings.

The Music Man will get "on the 1's and 2's" and attack the first ground vehicle to break through the ATVs. If the nearest foe is one in flight, the Music Man will hit it with The Drop.

GR notes: The Music Man controls the Escalade from his DJ booth on the platform at the back of the vehicle. It is currently on an auto-follow program which allows it to keep up with the rest of the caravan.

Pinhead will enter the fray, first taunting the players and attacking the next turn.

Pinhead

14ft Length, 6ft Width, 5ft Height, 3,300lbs., One Rider

Description: In 2032, Tanzeer, a car company, spun off of Resolv Corp and named after its late CEO Eli Tanzeer III, released its flagship model: the Tanzeeer Ladybug. This fully electric vehicle was the first to feature the new "Solar Cell" battery and was meant to give the driver a truly panoramic view of the road while allowing a small back cargo bed for storage. The Raiders version is less worried about the view and more concerned with inflicting pain on the rival bands.

1 Attack + 1 SA Per Turn

Somebody To Shove: DMG +1 Pinhead will purposefully ram itself into another vehicle its own size or smaller, attempting to run it off the road causing LP damage to their opponent and forcing them to make a **Guts Check** or suffer 1 **Guts Penalty**. On their next turn, the driver must make a **Brawn Check +2** to retain control of their vehicle or slide off the road taking environmental damage and losing their turn.

Punchbuggy Blue (Ice Slick): 1 Use, DMG +4 Pinhead breaks out ahead of the pack and releases a 10ft wide Ice Slick in its wake. Any vehicle that drives through it must make an **Action Check +2** to prevent hydroplaning. A failed check will result in the car crashing into the next nearest car, causing them both damage and 1 **Guts Penalty**. Drivers will start from the position of the wreck on their next turn.

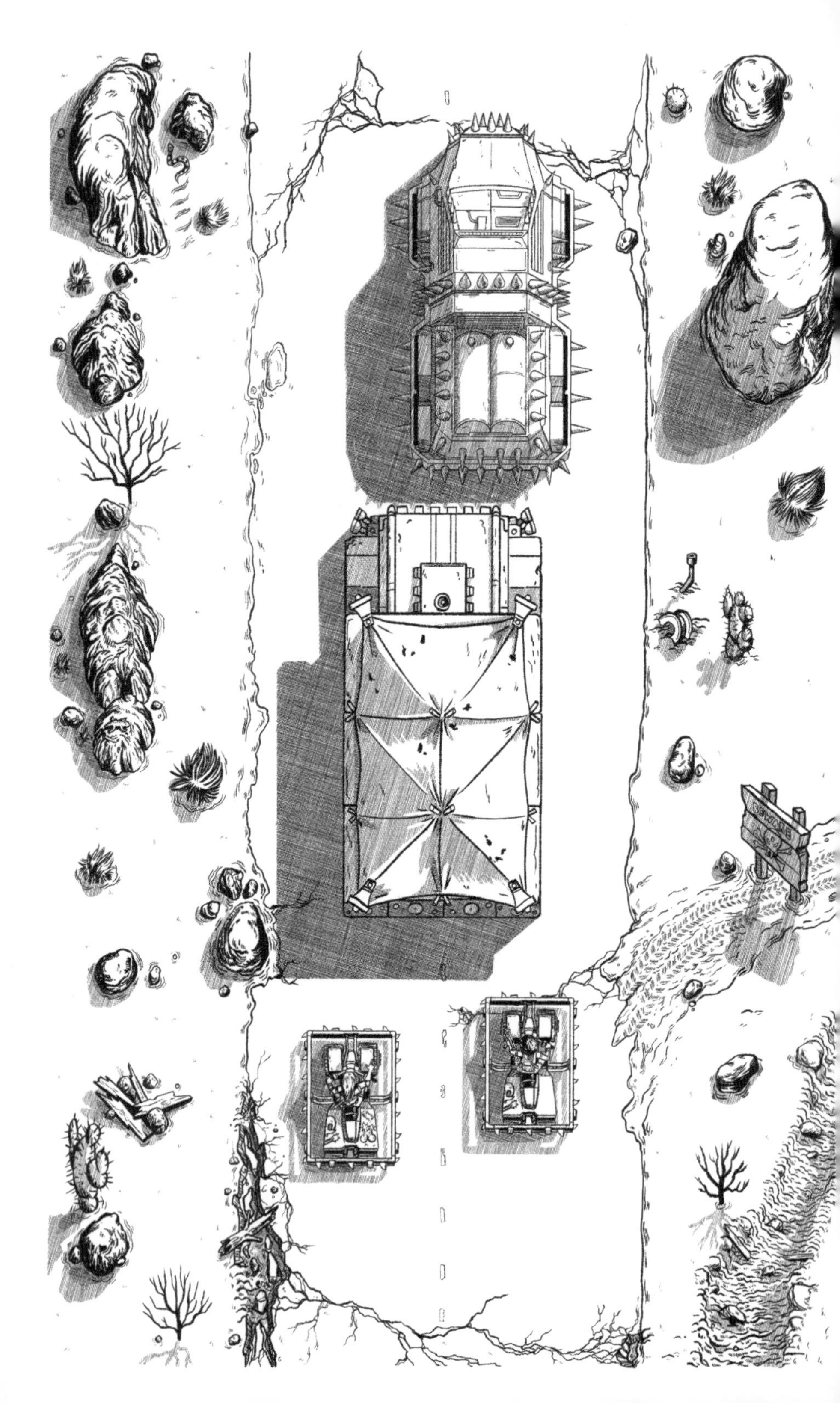
BEWARE

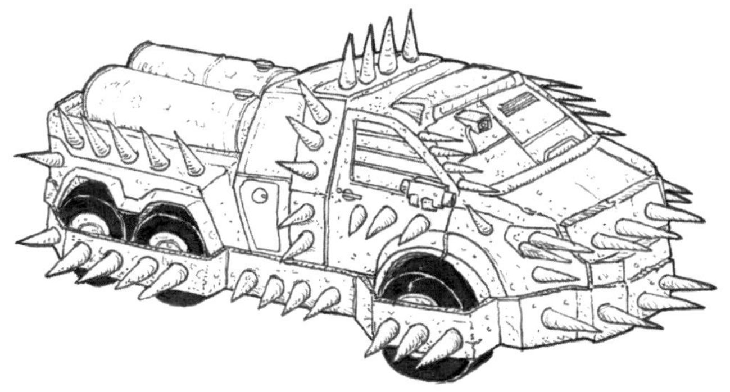

40 LP
Action 7
Brains
Brawn 7
Cool
Charm
Guts 7

Punchbuggy Red (Flame Thrower): 1 Use, DMG +5 When Pinhead has a car following close behind in the same lane it will shoot a flame from its tailpipe that will ignite the car's hood behind it, causing ongoing fire damage. The flaming car will continue to take 5 LP damage each turn and if it remains on fire it must make a **Guts Check** or suffer 1 **Guts Penalty**.

Special Ability - Hellriser II: DMG +6 If Pinhead finds itself between two enemy vehicles it will shoot out two spikes from its doors to attach itself via cables to each vehicle. Once both are pierced, Pinhead will slam on its brakes using its weight to yank back at the cables whipping the two vehicles and causing damage to both before releasing. Each car will take damage plus 1 **Guts Penalty**.

GR Notes: Pinhead is covered in spines, making it difficult to board. Every turn a player spends on Pinhead's exterior will result in 5 LP damage.

Combat Stage 2: The Music Man will unleash a Foam Party on the road to deal with anybody who tries to roll up on him and keep trying to fend off the air support with the Drop.

Pinhead and the ATVs will keep up their assault on the ground, trying to prevent them from reaching the Music Man.

GR Notes: This would be an excellent time to plant the seed in the player's mind that a tornado is in its organizing stage to the west of your location near O' Leary's farm.

Combat Stage 3 And Beyond: The ATVs will continue attacking until the enemy is dead or they are, with no exceptions. However, the Music Man and Pinhead both have a particular role in that when The Music Man's Escalade's Luck Points dip below half, or Pinhead is commandeered or destroyed, the second stage of the battle will be triggered.

When the second stage of the battle is triggered, read the following:

> The Music Man grabs the mic, "Oh boy, we got a Twister over here!"
>
> On the side of the highway, the perfect cone shape of a Twister appears in the dust.
>
> Music Man turns some knobs on deep bass, a frequency so low you can't hear it anymore, you just feel it in your bones. This sonic wave hits the twister and pushes it into your path.

Road Hazard: "Auntie Em, It's A Twister!" The Twister will affect all vehicles in its path except the Music Man, which will get slightly ahead and shape its path with a sonic wave.

All ground vehicles caught in the tornado's path will be making their **Action Checks** at a +1 penalty as they dodge debris, and all air vehicles will be at a +2

GR Notes: As far as road hazards go, a tornado is one that is a force of nature and is not to be taken lightly. It is also a little slice of pure chaos served up piping hot at the gaming table. Besides the obvious types of damage caused in its wake, you can throw whatever you can possibly think that it picked up in its path at the players; so why not get weird?

Large Cardboard Box Filled With 40 Neon Colored Pool Noodles: DMG -7

White Picket Fence: DMG -4

The Kitchen Sink: DMG 0 plus one **Guts Penalty**.

Mrs. O'Leary's Cow: DMG +5 plus one **Guts Penalty**.

GR Notes: Mrs. O'Leary's Cow, Beuford, should be considered indestructible and no harm should befall him.

Once the Music Man is defeated, read the following:

One final dub siren blares from the desert stage as the Music Man plays his final set. A feedback loop starts before the shreddings of the military-grade speakers and causes the power amps to explode.

Scene 3: Keylow Is A Liar!

On the highway in front of you is the semi.

"Eyes on our prize," Croc says in your helmet.

The latch flips then Keylow leans out the back of the trailer holding a megaphone, "While you were all out, we raided your home base and started wasting everybody. Bye-bye, Hellsings, one less band in the wasteland."

Croc yells over your headset, "We've been double-crossed! Death Point Raiders are attacking the camp. You'll never make it back in time. Go shut up Keylow, permanently!"

A jet of fire shoots past everyone. You can feel the heat cooking your skin.

The Naa Zaa has entered the battle.

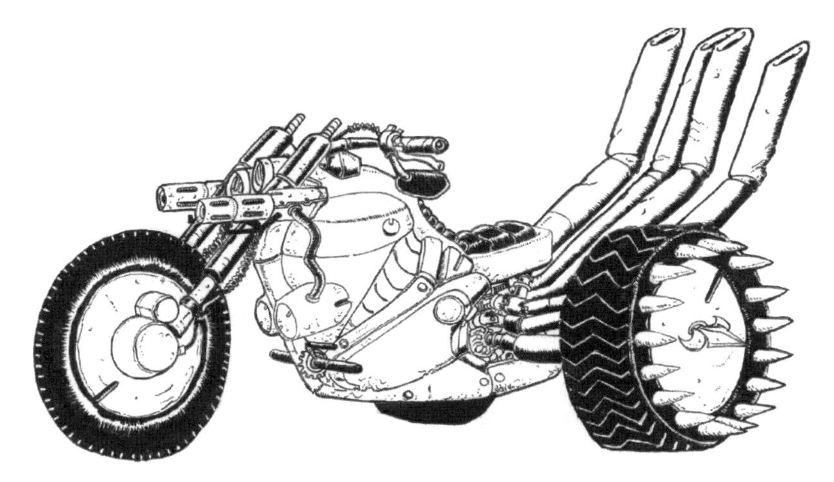

Naa Zaa's Motorcycle

9ft Length, 4ft Width, 6ft Height, 800lbs., One Rider

50 LP
Action 8
Brains
Brawn 6
Cool
Charm
Guts 7

Description: This three-wheel trike was custom-made by Bishop Motorsports as a showroom piece to celebrate the company's 10th anniversary. When the Dweebs discovered it on a raid in 2057 they thought it would be the perfect tribute for the Naa Zaa. He was so moved by the gift he mounted his prize flamethrower to it.

1 Attack + 1 SA Per Turn

Flame Thrower: 5 Round Tank, DMG +3 The Naa Zaa's motorcycle shoots 20ft long flames from its front fork engulfing anything it touches in bright orange fire.

Special Ability - Firestarter: This flame attack can affect multiple vehicles in a 10-foot area and will continue to burn to do an additional 3 LP damage for the next three turns unless extinguished.

GR Notes: This weapon cannot be reloaded.

Wheel Spikes: DMG 0 From the center of both the trikes, the back wheels protrude razor-sharp spikes in the shape of a fleur de lis. These spikes will ravage the sides of their opponent's vehicles and cause their opponent to make a **Guts Check** should they do full damage.

Combat Stage 1: The Naa Zaa will hang back towards the Semi and act as a defensive line for Low Key, firing his shotgun at the nearest enemy vehicle. Low Key will fire his shotgun at any airborne vehicles that try to fly over or past the Semi and any ground vehicle that breaks the Naa Zaa's defensive line.

GR notes: Once the Naa Zaa's bike drops below 10 Luck Points, he ditches it and jumps onto a player's vehicle, and starts to throw down.

Combat Stage 2: The Naa Zaa will shoot his flamethrower and attempt to engulf a single or multiple vehicles in flames and then fire his shotgun at the vehicle nearest him. If he can position himself between two equal-sized or smaller vehicles he will plow into one and then serpentine into the other using his wheel spikes.

Combat Stage 2 will continue until the Semi has been reduced to half its Luck Points.

Once the Semi drops to half its Luck, read the following:

> Low Key runs into the back and yells, "Now witness the true power of this Semi truck!"
>
> The top of the trailer explodes in the air and the sides pop off, revealing a ginormous excavator on the trailer's bed. Low Key is currently driving it. He uses the boom and the bucket to push a bunch of logs onto the road while screaming like a maniac.
>
> Meanwhile, you hear an explosion in your headset and Croc says, "Wolf blew a hole in their line. Boar is in the Bradley. We are making a run for it."

Hellcavator (Boss)

22ft Length, 15ft Width, 20ft Height, 20,000 lbs., One Rider

50 LP
Action 5
Brains
Brawn 9
Cool
Charm
Guts 8

Description: In the late 00s, the Nelson Trucking Company was the knot that held the roadways of the midwest together, delivering pallets of food and other goods exclusively in the center 13. This 2031 "Ricky" model was the creme de la creme of long haulers, fitted with top-of-the-line leather seating and a luxury sleeper. While many of the fleet made their way to the west coast at the start of the war, Nelson retained eleven trucks to service their routes until the company folded in 2042.

1 Attack + 1 SA Per Turn

Logjammin': 20 Logs, DMG +5 Once freed from the confines of the trailer, it will push giant logs onto the road causing damage to any vehicle they hit as well as 1 **Guts Penalty** and a +1 penalty to **Action Checks** until the end of the driver's next turn.

Digging Your Grave: DMG 0 The Hellcavator will swing its arm around to the nearest vehicle,

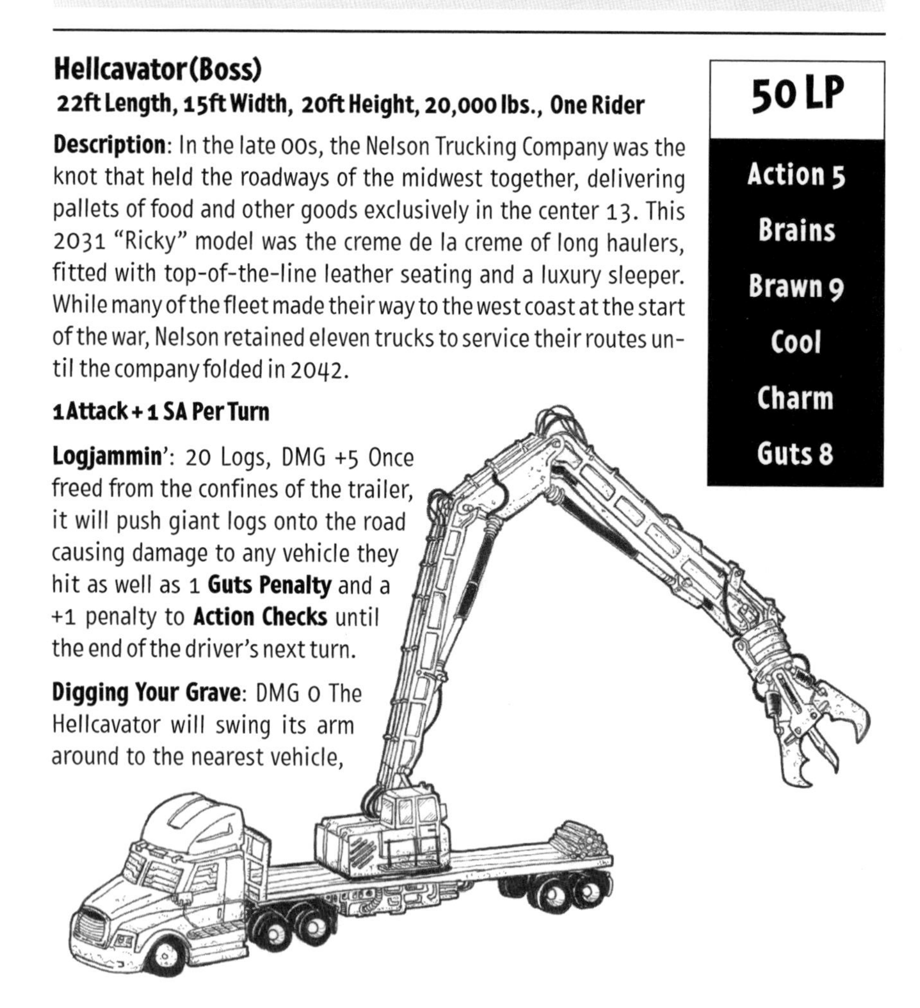

dig the bucket down at the vehicle's motor, and drag it back towards the roof. If it succeeds in incapacitating the vehicile it will result in a **Guts Penalty**.

Swing For The Fences: DMG -4 If there is a flying vehicle in range the Hellcavator will raise its arm and swing the bucket at the vehicle to swat it away, resulting in a **Guts Check +1**.

Cinder Block Surprise!: 15 Cinder Blocks, DMG -3 If there is a flying vehicle at a distance, the Hellcavator will pick up a cinder block in its bucket and launch it at the vehicle, which will result in a +2 penalty to **Action Checks** until the end of the pilots next turn.

Special Ability - Loser Leaves Town: The Hellcavator will reach its bucket down and try to rip a small to medium-sized vehicle off the road, instantly wasting the ride unless the driver makes a successful **Action Check +3**.

GR Notes: If the driver fails they may still make an **Action Check +1** to dive free of the vehicle as it gets launched into the wastelands.

Combat Stage 3 And Beyond: Key Low takes control of the excavator and will knock three logs onto the road, forcing all ground vehicles to make an **Action Check +2** or take damage plus 1 Guts Penalty. Then, if possible, the excavator will attack any flying vehicles. If the Naa Zaa is still alive at this point in the combat they will continue attacking the ground vehicles.

All enemies will continue attacking until their deaths.

Once the Naa Zaa and Key Low are dead, read the following:

> Croc says, "Some of us got away, some didn't. Meet up at the silo."

End Of The Episode Wrap Up And Awards Ceremony

As you wrap for the night or for a quick break before the next episode, have the players roll 1d10 to replenish Luck Points. They may always re-roll a 1. Remember there is **no maximum for Luck Points**. You can also do an **End of the Episode Award Ceremony**, letting the group vote and giving out awards for:

Best Action Sequence: +1 Luck Points

Best Commandeering: +2 Luck Points

Best Joke or One Liner: +3 Luck Points

Best Kill: +4 Luck Points

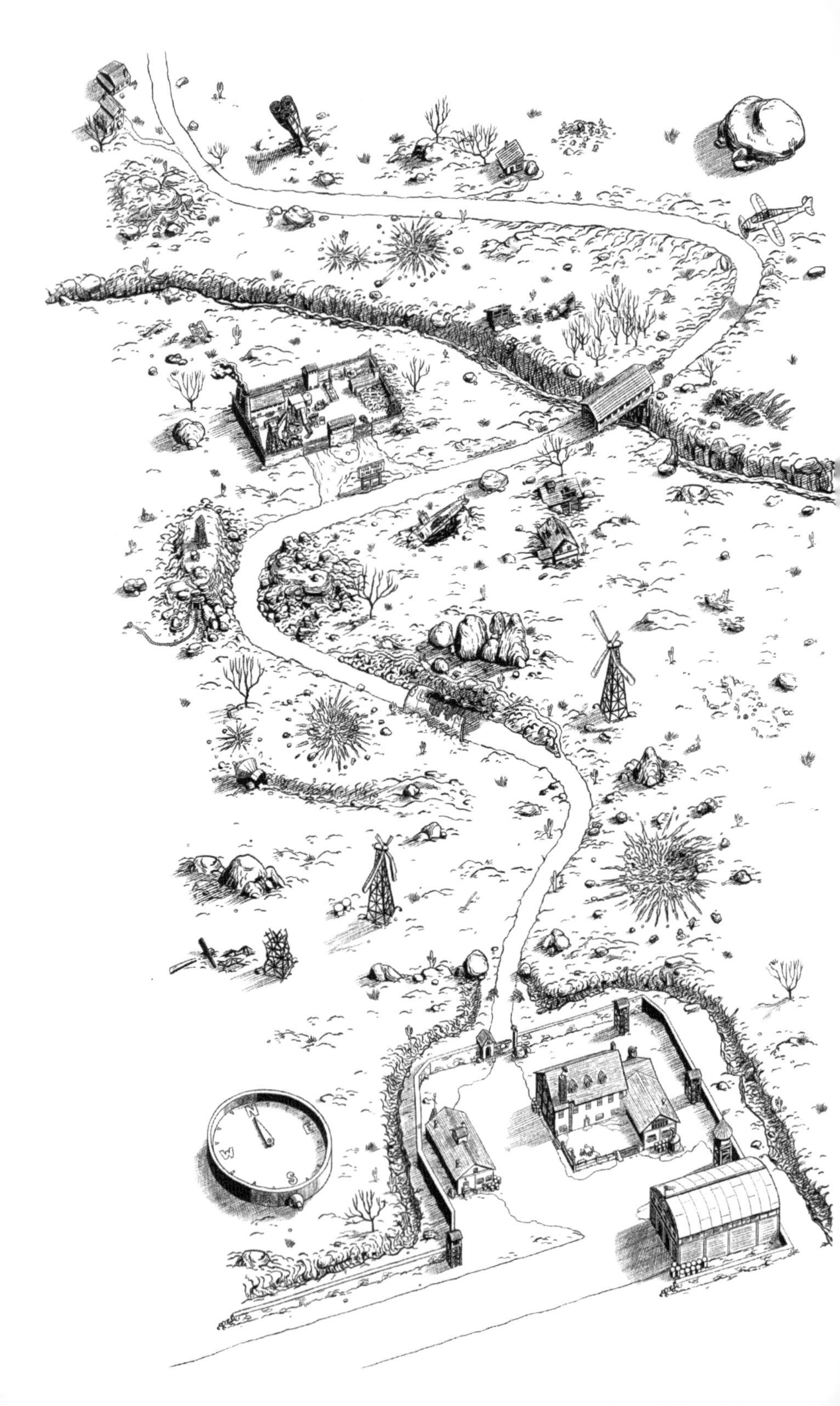
N
E
W
S

Episode 2: Night Moves

As you pull off the highway onto the darkened field, you see flashing lights from the roof of an old silo.

Croc's exhausted voice comes over your headsets.

"Welcome home, pack."

You are greeted by Bee when you pull up. Bee is the Hellsing quartermaster and he always makes sure the hive is running right. He's 5'3", made of skin, bones, and charisma.

"Thank the wastes you're all right," he says.

"We're trying to put together what happened. People scurried after Wolf sacrificed herself. You should have seen her. Her helmet gleamed in the sunlight as she drove that ammo truck right into a pack of Raiders, and "poof"! She made Kansas shake. Then Boar took the Bradley and blasted a path. We grabbed the orphans and made a run for it.

Croc is on the lookout; he's been trying to contact anyone missing. Who knows how much luck he is having? Just between us, Croc's not lookin' too hot. But he gets stubborn, so there's no getting him to rest until he feels he is done."

"But listen up, we got a "right now" problem. We didn't think about leaving anything behind when we ditched this place. Bear is working on getting the power running again, but we need food. There just ain't enough sluice* for everyone. Word has it a small band, the Blue Dragons, raided a military truck carrying supplies to the coast. Word has it they are getting fat on MREs. So how about you glide into their camp and steal back what's ours."

GR Notes: Sluice is the sugar water run off of batteries as they recharge. You can drink it, which will help keep you alive, but that's about it.

Bee gives the players a rough map of the Blue Dragons' base. It's an old farmhouse with a large aluminum shed on the property.

The mission is to glide in. Maximum stealth is necessary since, even though Blue Dragons are clowns, there is no way you could take on that many of them head on. You must sneak through the base and steal the supply truck out from under their noses.

If the players dawdle, Bee says they are burning moonlight and need to do this mission quickly. Otherwise they will have to wait until tomorrow night and people will start to starve. If asked, Bee says there are about twenty Blue Dragons. They also have a reputation for having a lot of firepower.

Hang Glider (Wind Powered)

18ft Length, 2ft Width, 24ft Wingspan, 5ft Height, 60lbs., One Rider / 1 Upgrade Slot

No attacks

Description: This air-powered single rider hang glider is explicitly designed for silent infiltra-

5 LP	
Action 5	Cool
Brains	Charm
Brawn 2	Guts 2

tion and has no onboard weaponry. It's also dangerous and not recommended for riders under 5ft tall.

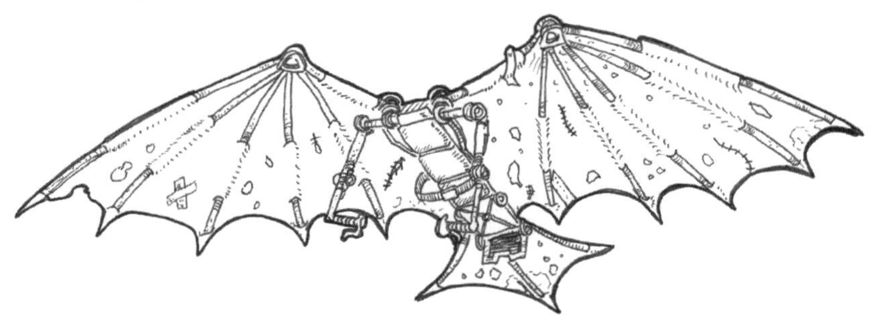

Scene 1: A Little B & E

You glide silently through the night air to a ridge overlooking the Blue Dragon farm. You recognize a lot of it from Bee's map. The front yard has a bunch of motorcycles and ATVs lined up. On the farmhouse's roof is a sniper leaning against the chimney who looks asleep. Two Dragons on watch sit around a rickety card table playing poker and drinking bottles of fermented sluice in the yard. There is a big telephone pole nearby with a siren on top. The rest of the lights in the house are out. You see the big shed on the other side of the property with a military truck sticking out.

The players can decide how they want to get to the truck.

1A) Sniper nest

1B) Card table

1C) Hanger

1D) Garage

1A) Sniper Nest - In the distance, leaning against the chimney of the house, is a sniper quite literally sleeping on the job. He is not trying to hide his location, and as you glide in you can hear him snoring loudly into the night air.

Upon their descent into the ridge, players must make a successful **Action Check +2** to land quietly. If any team member fails, they will take 3 LP damage and 1 Guts Penalty. This failure will also result in **2 Blue Dragons** performing a perimeter sweep around the grounds looking for where the sound originated.

Once the players land, ditch their gliders and reach the perimeter, they may make a **Brains Check +2** to disable the perimeter trip wire set to the alarm. If the alarm is disabled, they can do whatever they want as long as it doesn't make enough noise to wake the sniper. If he wakes, he will immediately begin firing on the players.

The Sniper: If the sniper is abruptly woken up, he will take his first shot at half damage as he will be firing wildly. Any subsequent attack will be at full damage.

The Alarm: If the alarm is tripped, the players will have one turn to make it to the shed so they can hotwire the Truck, which is a **Brains Check +3**.

Within two turns of the alarm tripping, **15 Blue Dragons** will pour out of the house and open fire on anyone and everyone who is not a gang member.

GR Notes: Players should not be subjected to checks unless they are doing something that would provoke one, i.e. opening a door or window, walking up a flight of stairs, or climbing onto an object or building. Should any activity fall within these lines, have the players make an **Action Check** with the appropriate bonus or penalty.

1B) Card Table - Around the back of the house there is an open-air wooden patio with a barbecue grill and a picnic table. There are two Blue Dragons loudly playing a heated game of poker. You can hear them slurring their speech. You can tell a couple of things from being within earshot of these two. One, their names are Boyd and Dan. Two, they aren't very good at cards.

The **2 Blue Dragons** sitting at the table playing poker, Boyd, and Dan, are supposed to be guarding the hangar but got drunk on Sluiceshine instead.

Boyd is twitchy and will begin firing his sub-machine gun at any sound so that any stealth maneuvering will require an **Action Check +2**.

Dan is kind of crazy. If Boyd is alerted, Dan's first impulse is to throw the jug of Sluiceshine at the players and then shoot at it, creating an exploding fireball. Any players within 5 feet of the explosion will take 2 LP damage and must make a **Guts Check** or receive **1 Guts Penalty**.

If Boyd and Dan should enter combat with the players, they will both attack with sub-machine guns. **3 Blue Dragons** will start firing handguns out the window on the next turn, and **5 Blue Dragons** will come from around the front of the house and enter combat the turn after. Combat will continue until all are dead or the players escape.

1C) The Hanger - The hangar is a 100 x 100 aluminum shed. There is a huge padlock on the front double doors. Rusting signs hang on the walls, with messages such as: "Do Not Enter", "Property of Dudley", and "Smile! You're On Camera".

In the hangar is a powder blue Supermarine Spitfire. It has a full Blue Dragon paint job, and it's been retrofitted with Carbon Plus power. It's in beautiful, pristine condition. The players will not be able to fly the Spitfire in this encounter.

It requires three people to wheel it out of the garage and another in the pilot seat to get it in the air. There is also an infrared alarm set up so that anyone other than the pilot who enters the cockpit will trigger it. The Blue Dragons would have discovered and begun shooting at the party by that time.

GR Notes: The Spitfire will take four people to get it into the air, with no exceptions. If the players want to try this, you may want to allude to this being a death trap.

If the players decide to sabotage the plane, it will result in a **-1 bonus** to their **Action Checks** against their interactions with the Spitfire during the boss fight and an ongoing **1 LP** damage reduction from its attacks.

1D) The Garage - You hear a crappy radio playing some loud crunchy music, you make out some of the lyrics something about "And Those Hollywood nights, in those Hollywood Hills".

There's a big military truck with its doors wide open. The back is filled to the brim with wooden cases labeled MREs. On top, there is a gun turret with two 50-caliber machine guns.

There is also a Dune Buggy complete with a harpoon gun attached to the back and two motorcycles charging.

A Blue Dragon mechanic is currently underneath a car raised on a floor jack.

Nick DiFabbio, the Blue Dragon mechanic, is lying on a creeper underneath a car and is hard at work. You can hear the muffled sounds of him singing along, missing most of the words in the verse but going hard on the chorus. His calves and combat boots are the only things visible.

Nick is pretty oblivious to the players entering the garage unless they make an unruly amount of noise. He is easy to sneak up on due to how focused he is on his work. Players will have to either charm or subdue him if they want to steal the truck. He is pretty cowardly and will go along with whatever the players want. One player may make a **Charm Check +1** to keep Nick calm. If successful, Nick will raise his hands, wince, and say, "just please don't hurt me". A failure will result in Nick feeling threatened. He will start crying out for help or sounding an alarm if he thinks he is going to be taken hostage.

GR Notes: If one of the players decides to kick out the jack and drop the car on Nick, he will scream bloody murder and the Blue Dragons will be on the scene, guns drawn, within seconds.

Hot Wheels: The team needs an exit strategy and can hotwire the truck, motorcycle, and Dune Buggy with a **Brains Check +2**. The truck is loud and once its engine fires up it will alert the guards playing poker (should they not have been previously dealt with), causing them to investigate in two turns. They will arrive with machine guns drawn.

GR Notes: If the players search the garage before attempting to hotwire any vehicles, they will discover an unlocked lock box on the wall with keys for everything in the garage.

"Beulah"

Blue Dragon Supply Truck 23ft Length, 8ft Width, 9ft Height, 4,000 lbs., 8 Riders

Description: When the military pulled out of Fort Dillon and headed west at the start of the war, they left a skeleton crew on base mostly to do supply runs to those left behind during the day and keep watch at night. Beulah got caught up in a firefight between the Death Point Raiders and the Hexies while on a supply run and was abandoned by her driver. She has since been rehomed and made a part of the Blue Dragon family.

1 Attack

.50 Caliber Mounted Gun: 100 Rounds, DMG 0

40 LP
Action 5
Brains
Brawn 7
Cool
Charm
Guts 6

Barf Bag"
Blue Dragon Motorcycle With Sidecar

Motorcycle: 7ft Length, 3ft Width, 4ft Height, 390 lbs., 1 Rider

Sidecar: 6ft Length, 2ft Width, 3ft Height, 120 lbs., 1 Rider

Description:This street bike was one of the vehicles left behind when the military pulled out of Fort Dillon, as it was deemed unnecessary for the war effort. In its heyday it was primarily used to cart high-ranking officers and guests around the compound. Rumor has it, former Vice President Mike Green barfed all over the sidecar while being transported to a photo op!

1 Attack or 1 SA Per Turn: Driver and Passenger

15/5 LP
Action 8
Brains
Brawn 3
Cool
Charm
Guts 4

Scene 2: First Stretch

The dirt road leading from the farmhouse is a little worse for wear; there are some downed trees and a single empty toll booth-style checkpoint. You hear machine gunfire behind you.

Have the truck driver make an **Action Check +1** to make the hard turn onto the highway and a **Brawn Check +1** to slam through the wooden checkpoint. The truck will still barrel through the checkpoint but receive a **1 Guts Penalty** if they fail.

Once on the highway, two motorcycles with sidecars speed up next to your truck. One of the drivers yells for you to pull over.

Do you?

Combat Stage 1: Two Blue Dragons motorcycles, each with a rider and a passenger in the sidecar, will race up to the supply truck and attempt to get the driver to pull over before attempting to commandeer it.

Driver Side Motorcycle: If the driver fails to heed their request, the driver-side biker will ride parallel to the truck and have their sidecar gunner fire at it. Their attack is meant to draw the driver's attention away from the passenger-side motorcycle, not to destroy the truck and its cargo.

Passenger Side Motorcycle: The driver of the passenger side motorcycle will attempt to board the truck through the passenger side door (letting the sidecar rider take over the driving duties). If a passenger is present, they will attempt to kill or rip them out of the seat, launching them onto the road and then attacking the driver.

Both motorcycle riders will fire their sidearms back at enemy vehicles attempting to approach from the rear during the first stretch before breaking the formation.

Scene 3: Second Stretch

As you speed down the highway, the moon is bright in the sky. Even with the headlights of the supply truck it's hard to see ahead of you in the looming darkness. A bright light hits your side view mirror, nearly blinding you. The giant floodlight on top of a Greyhound Armored Vehicle is speeding up after you.

"Clown Car"

Blue Dragon Light Armored Car - 16ft Length, 8ft Width, 8ft Height, 17,400 lbs., 6 Riders

Description: TDudley picked up the Clown Car a few years into the war from a disgruntled lieutenant who had been quietly "liberating" military supplies during Fort Dillon's deployment to the west coast. He nicknamed this Light Armored vehicle the "Clown Car" because even with its weapons it still seats four, albeit uncomfortably, inside (Commander, Loader, Gunner Driver, Assistant Driver) and has space for two more on the back platform. The Clown Car's six wheels make it optimal for country driving and maneuverability.

100 LP
Action 6
Brains
Brawn 8
Cool
Charm
Guts 8

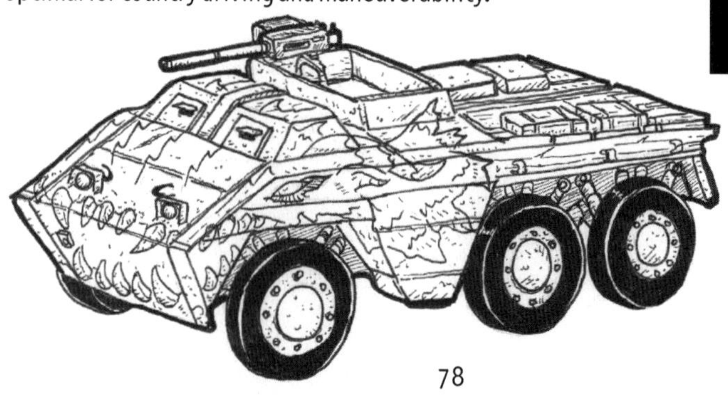

1 Attack Per Member of the Crew + 1 SA

Special Ability - "The Big Gun" 37mm Repeating Cannon: 6 Rounds, DMG +3 This cannon has armor piercing ammunition and it will result in damage plus 1 **Guts Penalty** for any vehicle hit by one of its rounds.

Combat Stage 2: Two warning shots will be fired by the **Light Armored Car** when it enters combat to slow down the truck. These shots will create giant potholes, requiring the truck and other Hellsing vehicles to make an **Action Check +1** or take **3 LP** damage and **1 Guts Penalty**.

It will continue to fire its cannon at the Hellsings riders from a distance, aiming for the smaller vehicles first while its teammates attempt to commandeer the truck.

GR Notes: The Blue Dragons will try to save the truck full of MREs; however, if faced with the option of losing their cargo or destroying it, they will opt to destroy it.

GR Notes: If the players managed to trash or sabotage any motorcycles in the garage or front yard, this encounter is just with the armored vehicle. If it comes to that, and the armored vehicle is attacking by itself, the armored vehicle will go straight for the kill. If the players did not sabotage the motorcycles they will face an additional **2 Blue Dragon Motorcycles**.

Scene 4: Aces High

> As you get closer to the **Silo**, your new home base, you need to cross an old wooden covered bridge about 100 feet over a river. On the other side is a blockade, two Dragon-clad police cruisers parked perpendicular, with two Blue Dragons aiming rifles over the hoods.

Ramming Speed: If the truck attempts to ram through the barricade, it must make a successful **Brawn Check +3**. A failure will result in **10 LP** damage and **1 Guts Penalties** for the supply truck. The squad cars will be wasted regardless of the outcome.

GR Notes: If the supply truck fails to make it through the barricade, its enemies will get a +2 bonus to damage on their next attack turn. The truck must make a **Brawn Check +3** on its next turn to push through the blockade and keep driving. It must make a **Guts Check** or receive another **Guts Penalty**.

Once the supply truck is through the blockade or fully stopped at the blockade and stuck in a shootout, the boss fight will be triggered.

Read the following:

> As the sun makes a feeble attempt to rise on the horizon, beginning to illuminate the dust clouds heavy in the sky, you hear a sound like a chainsaw go by. Everyone looks up just in time to see the whirling blades of a P-47 Warhawk as it roars through the clouds.

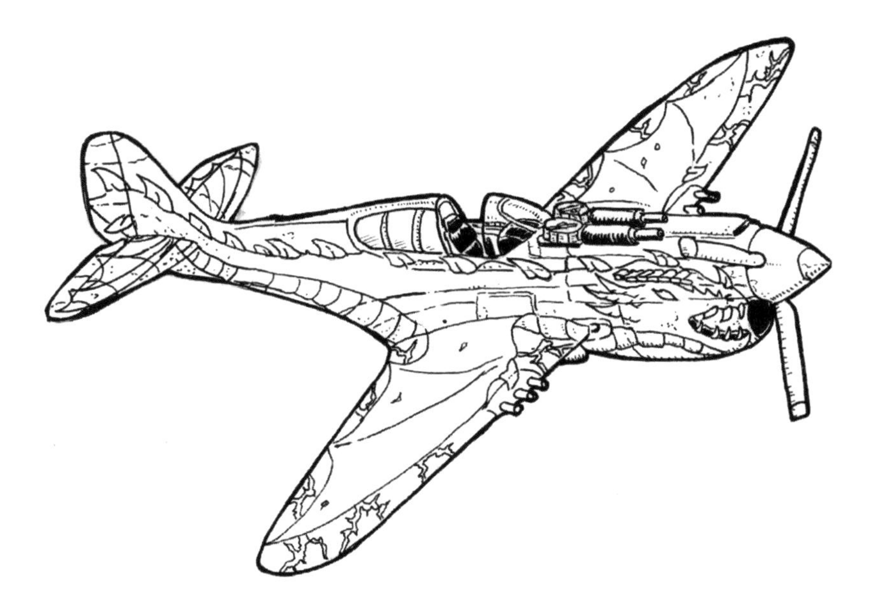

"Dragonheart"

Blue Dragons Fighter Plane - Length 12ft, 36ft Wingspan, 30ft Height, 9,100 lbs., Fuselage 60 LP / Wing 30 LP / Cockpit 8 LP, 1 Rider

60 LP 30 LP 8 LP
Action 8
Brains
Brawn 7
Cool
Charm
Guts 6

Description:Before the Amphikura War, this 1944 P-47 Warhawk had come out of retirement for one last flight at the Great Bend Barnstormer's Benefit-Charity Event before making its way to its final resting place at the Aviation Museum in Wichita. Originally painted army green, it has since been stylized with a Blue Dragon, Dudley's call sign from back in his military days. It has been updated to Carbon +, giving it triple the horsepower it had when it ran on a more traditional fuel source.

1 Attack or 1 SA

Bullet Strafe: The Blue Dragons Fighter Plane will swoop in for a single attack every turn doing 6 LP damage to every player and creature in combat unless they can make a successful **Action Check +3**.

Special Ability - The Bomb That Will Bring Us Together: 2 Bombs, DMG +5 Dudley took the cosmetic casings of the 250lb bombs attached to Warhawk and stuffed every explosive he could find lying around inside them. While it may not pack the same punch as the original, it will still deal DMG +5 and **1 Guts Penalty** to any vehicle within a 20ft radius of its impact.

GR Notes: Only one bomb may be dropped per turn.

Combat Stage 3 And Beyond: When the Hellsings turn along the curve towards the highway exit, the Dragons will open fire.

he Warhawk will use its **Bullet Strafe attack** every turn, doing **6 LP** damage to every player and/or vehicle in combat unless they can make a successful **Action Check +3** to dodge out of the way.

Every other turn, it will drop one of its bombs aimed at an area where it can cause the most damage and injure the most people.

Once the P-47 is defeated, read the following:

> You pull up to the Silo and are greeted by the rest of the Hellsings. Your timing is impeccable, Bear has just managed to get the place powered up and running. Everybody is happy, the lights are on, and Croc says you saved the day. He promotes you all to lieutenants.
>
> Bee hops out of the back of the truck and says, "Hey, this truck didn't just have MREs."
>
> He pops open a pelican case on the ground and lifts up a shiny new rocket launcher.

End Of The Episode Wrap Up And Awards Ceremony

As you wrap for the night or a quick break before the next episode, have the players roll 1d10 to replenish Luck Points. They may always re-roll a 1. Remember, there is **no maximum for Luck Points**. You can also do an **End of the Episode Award Ceremony**, letting the group vote, giving out awards for:

Best Action Sequence: +1 Luck Points

Best Commandeering: +2 Luck Points

Best Joke or One Liner: +3 Luck Points

Best Kill: +4 Luck Points

Earn Your Stripes Bonus: +5 Luck Points

Catch You Next Time!

Episode 3: Bear's Quest

You wake up the following day after a fun party in your honor and look out the window of the Silo. It doesn't look half bad outside. Everybody is walking around, doing their own thing. You see Bee surrounded by some younglings standing in front of a chalkboard. Croc is hanging by a picnic table drinking from a French press with Fox and Crow. Bear is in the garage, sparking her acetylene torch with her welding helmet on.

The players can pick and choose from one of the following three activities. Let them know that everyone milling about is super excited to see them.

3A) Bee teaching

3B) Croc table

3C) Bear garage

3A) Bee is surrounded by the younglings and you are immediately overwhelmed by kids looking for autographs when you walk by.

"Alright, leave the heroes alone and let's get back to today's lesson. Who here can tell me about the Kansas City Sounds?" Bee asks.

One astute and brown-nosing kid responds, "Kansas City Sounds was the recording studio where The Hellsings recorded their hit record, Sunset Blood Driver, which was also the name of their first single, which hit 23 on the Billboard charts."

The rest of the kids boo when they hear the phrase "Billboard charts".

"That's right, Johan," Bee says, "Hey, let's talk later. You might be distracting the kids a bit."

Bee then continues with the lesson about the band The Hellsings.

It becomes pretty apparent that your presence around the kids is distracting. Bee says, "There will be plenty of time later for questions if the party hangs around." There is nothing else helpful in this area.

3B) As you approach Croc, he greets you warmly. Everybody gets a hug before he offers you a seat at the picnic table.

"You guys did an awesome thing last night. Everyone here was worried. They thought it was the end but you brought back some light. Funny how a win and some good food can change a mood."

The players can talk to Croc and ask him questions.

Croc's Rumor Table

1) Death Point Raiders were making waves and looking to take over the wasteland. That probably upset some people.

2) We're laying low until we get this place operational and lay down some roots.

3) I heard some noise late last night, but I wasn't sure if I had a nightmare about the raid. It was hard to fall asleep.

4) Kansas City Sounds is the Mecca for the band. Once this smoke clears, we're going to take a field trip.

5) The Hellsings will never get anywhere until we get some big rides. Some real big rides.

6) I don't know how to really put it; The Hellsing's music made everything make sense. Like my world clicked into place. I knew where I needed to be and what I needed to do.

7) The Black Swans are the biggest band in the waste, so big they don't even notice smaller bands unless they make a ruckus. They have so many heads but nobody's seen their leader Mrs. Olivia in years.

8) I was an enforcer for the Black Swan. I did it for a few years but I was miserable and I needed to get out. It wasn't easy to get out and sometimes I worry I never really did.

9) We still haven't heard from Boar. I hope he's okay. If Death Point took one of us prisoner, I know Boar would be giving them the biggest headache.

10) The rest of the countries are all worried about the war with the Amphikura. We are forgotten.

3C) You see Bear is in the middle of the garage working on a car's engine when she yells and slams the hood. The windshield shatters under the sudden onslaught. She rages and punches her cybernetic hand right through the car's grill.

She says something unintelligible and then takes a deep breath.

"Hey, come here, I need a favor. Cub left on a bike earlier with that blasted rocket launcher. He said he was looking to get revenge on the Death Point Raiders. He's looking to take out one of their outposts. Croc wants to cool down this feud with the Raiders. You need to stop Cub before he stirs up more trouble. He's young and dumb and in way over his head."

Bear cracks her knuckles and looks pensives for a moment. "I put a tracker on his bike because I don't trust him. You can use it to find him. I can outfit your vehicles however you want. Let's just hurry."

Bear's Vehicle Upgrades

All Terrain Tires
Auto Pilot
Bladed Pincers
Front Fork Slingshot
Grappling Hook
Morbius Brick
Nitro Booster
Oil Slick
Rocket Launcher
Twin Machine Guns

All-Terrain Tires: -1 bonus to **Action Checks**

Auto Pilot: Vehicle will drive or fly itself for two turns while the driver or pilot is occupied

Bladed Pincers: -1 to **Brawn Checks** / DMG -5

Front Fork Slingshot: (Motorcycle only) Can launch Grenades or Smoke Bombs

Grappling Hook: -2 to **Action Checks** when commandeering

Morbius Brick: Emergency reserve power. 10 LP

Nitro Booster: +1 penalty to **Action Checks** / -3 damage reduction (2 turns)

Oil Slick: Anyone in its wake will receive a +2 penalty to their **Action Checks**

Rocket Launcher: 1 Round / DMG +2

Twin Machine Guns: 30 Rounds / DMG -2

Scene 1: Milk Run

The tracker leads you to a field off of a quiet country road. In the center of this field are the smoldering remains of a motorcycle. The front end has been ripped off and is about 50 feet away. Cub tried to get away, his treads cut deep into the dirt, but larger tracks surrounded him on all sides. Now just the smell of burning rubber, metal, and plastic is all that remains of what happened.

There is one more thing you find. Mysterious puddles of something that looks like red ooze pool nearby.

If the players try to do detective work they will discover the following:

Cub was riding hot to the outpost and not paying attention to his surroundings when The Meat Grinders ambushed him. The leader, **Borgir**, pulled out in front of him in her monster truck, the **Murder Hearse**. Cub tried to escape but Borgir cut him off with her **GoreGun**, firing red ooze. **Blasphemizer** fired a harpoon and tore off the front of the bike. **CrushFace** lifted Cub and tossed him into its prison compactor. With that taken care of, they headed off for a good time at the Resolv Corp Center.

Your headsets crackle to life and you hear Bear swear.

"Damn it, we just heard an announcement over the radio. Cub is to be killed on display at the Resolv Corp Center unless the Hellsings meet the Slaughter Sisters Derby Challenge," Bear says.

"You got a chance to get him back. The Resolv Corp Center has rules. If you accept the challenge, it's you versus the Slaughter Sisters to settle whatever disputes they might have. No one else can interfere. It's our best shot. I don't know what I'll do if I can't beat Cub's reckless ass to death myself!"

GR Notes: The players can talk to Bear about this but she'll pull out the big guns if they hesitate to rescue Cub. Full tears!

Scene 2: All Murder, All Guts, All Fun

The Resolv Corp Center is infamous. It's where clans come to settle scores in front of an audience and tonight the parking lot is full. There's tailgating all over, barbecuing, drinking sluiceshine, but each different band keeps to themselves. Everyone knows the Black Swans run the Resolv Corp Center. Scores are settled in the Arena. If someone steps out of line or breaks the rules, the Black Swans will take care of them (and "by them" they mean their whole band). History has been erased by the Black Swans before.

Heavy netting covers the stands inside the Arena, but that doesn't stop people from trying to throw things onto the track. Or, vice versa, from stray shrapnel hitting the crowd. No one seems to mind. It's all for entertainment.

You see a man on a dais holding a microphone as you enter. He's dressed in a silver suit that reflects the spotlight in a blinding way, like a sentient disco ball.

"Tonight we have something special which will not disappoint! A direct challenge! The Meat Grinders, the sickest band in all of Kansas, versus The Hellsings, the newest kids on the block. Don't let their freshness fool you, they have been making a little noise lately."

"Hellsings! The Slaughter Sisters have something of yours. Would you like to take it back?"

A big screen shows Cub in a cage suspended high above the track.

"Well, would you?" He asks.

GR Notes: If the players don't accept the challenge the Slaughter Sisters attack anyway, except now with a second combat stage with extra rodeo "clown" gang motorcycles.

If the group responds "yes", read the following:

"Excellent," says the Man in the Silver Suit.

"Then, without further ado, ladies and gentlemen, I give you Borgir, leader of the Meat Grinders, in her Murder Hearse!"

The dark gates open to the north, spewing smoke like a demon maw. The thunderous rumble of a huge engine shakes the ground beneath you as an all-black coffin shaped monster truck rolls through. An A chord on an electric guitar wails over the speakers as an imposing figure slowly rises from the casket on the top of the vehicle. Seven feet tall, decked out in leather and steel and wearing a corset covered in menacing spikes, they are an avenging valkyrie from your darkest nightmares. They pull out a huge cannon connected to the casket by a hose and fire off a spew of offal and bone into the crowd. The smart ones who have been here before are wearing plastic raincoats and cheer when the unfortunate newbs in the audience scream as the toxic spew burns their flesh.

"Next up we have Tuuala, a lieutenant in the Blaphemizer!"

The gate to the west opens with a booming sound of cannon fire. A truck rolls through that looks frankensteined together from mismatched parts and features two rows of devil horn gun barrels. The engine revs again and another volley of fire explodes in the night sky.

"And finally, Azraph, the Meat Grinder's Master of Arms in the Crushface."

The gate to the east opens and a flattened car flies through and lands halfway up the course. Something that sounds like a cross between a lion's snarl and an engine roar echoes through the Arena as a reddish-brown monster truck springs forward and lands on its back wheels. Two mechanical arms at its side clamp shut loudly on the flattened car as the rear compactor begins to close. You hear the dying screams of the poor soul who was trapped inside.

"Well, someone is not getting a refund for tonight's event," says the Man in the Silver Suit to a raucous roar from the crowd. "Bye bye Gavy, the last of the Forsaken Assassins..."

Arena Rules

ReSolv Center: The old ReSolv Center was home to the 2036 World Series Champion Kansas City Scarecrows up until the start of the Amphikura Wars. The last event held at the arena was the Hot Rod Energy Drink's Monster's Ball. The floor remained untouched until the Man in the Silver Suit removed most of the floor seats, expanding the battlefield to create more of a Thunderdome effect.

Although the track is meant to run clockwise as far as the flow of traffic is intended, in this fanatical free for all anything goes in the name of carnage. The preferred method of conduct in the area is basic; drivers should do whatever possible to destroy their target, which means, in no uncertain terms, drive over whatever is in your way in any direction you please. There are only two rules in the arena. 1. Entertain the fans at all costs. 2. Try not to die.

GR Notes: Unbeknownst to the players, the only caveat to the "anything goes" style of driving is the exit ramp to the Party Pit. Should a driver try to enter the Party Pit ramp from the exit, their tires will meet the business end of the one-way **Tire Spikes** the Man in the Silver Suit had installed there as a gag. Any player or enemy vehicle that should drive across them will immediately take 5 LP damage and **2 Guts Penalties** and be stuck there for one turn.

Monster Truck Push Rules: Each arena section features different road hazards unknown to the players until they are activated. Each monster truck has a special ability that allows them to push any smaller vehicle into one of the hazards.

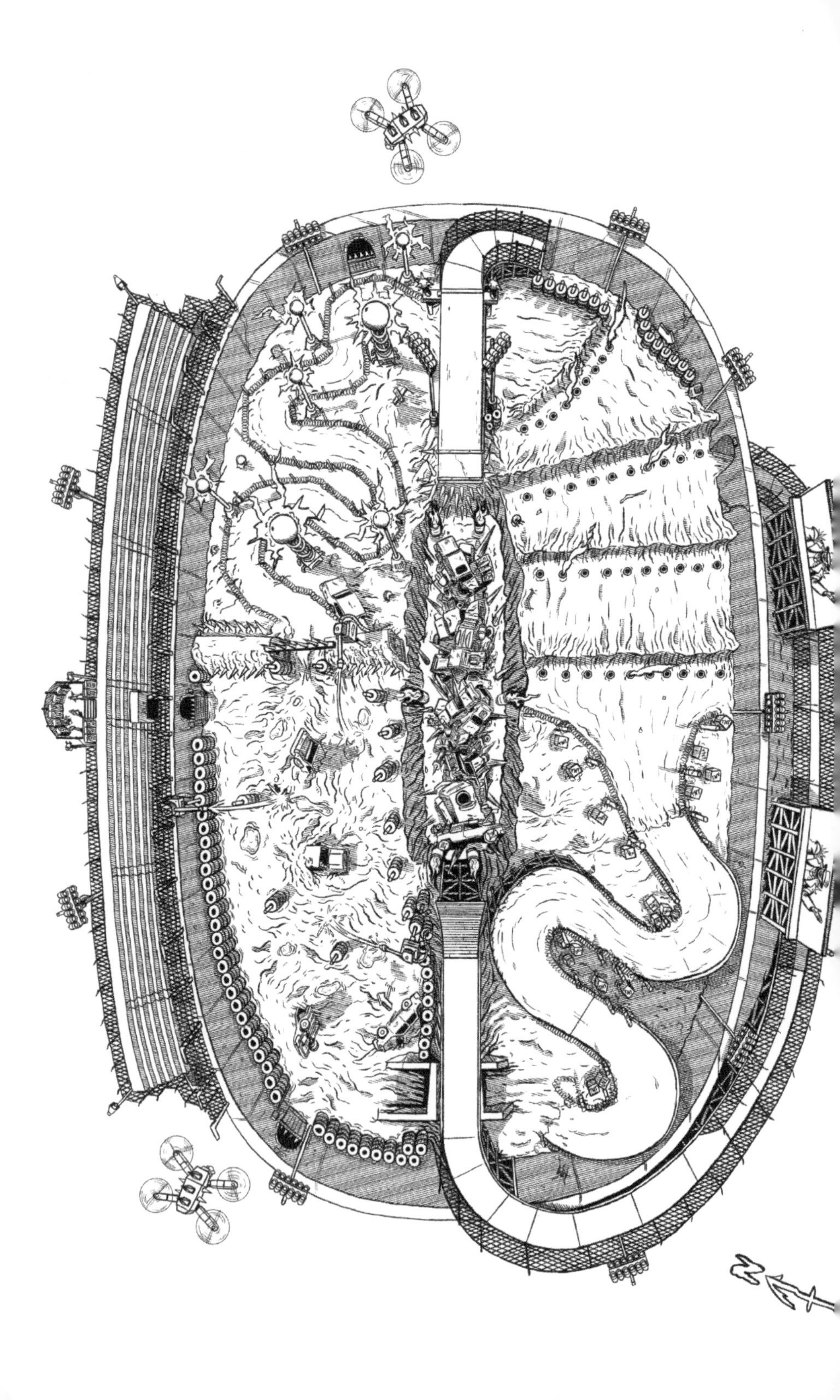

A) North West Section: Firehose / Mud Pit - When the riders pass this turn, fire hoses will blast them with water, making them fishtail in the mud. Players must make an **Action Check +1** or receive an additional +1 penalty to their next **Action Check**.

B) North East Section: Barbed Wire / Tesla Coil - Coming around this bend, players must make an **Action Check +1** or slide into the barbed wire while taking 3 LP damage. They must make a **Brawn Check +1** to break free or the Tesla Coil will shock them as they drive away, resulting in an additional 2 LP damage and 1 **Guts Penalty**.

C) South East Section: Mini Ramps / Pyro - When either gang uses the Mini Ramps, they must make an **Action Check +1** to stick the landing or a +2 if they are attempting to land on an enemy vehicle. If they should fail, the pyro will be set off and they will incur 5 LP damage.

D) South West Section: Exploding Barbed Wire - As the riders pass this section, they'll notice the ground has a decline making it easier to slide towards the exploding barbed wire. The players must make a successful **Action Check +2** or find themselves slamming into the corner and setting off an explosion resulting in 10 LP damage, **1 Guts Penalty**, and a -1 penalty to their next **Action Check**.

E) Party Pit: The ramp leading to the party pit is an outside track that starts at an off-ramp between the South East and West sections. To gain access, a rider must make an **Action Check +3** and if successful they will slot into this outside course which lets out between the North West and South West section of the track.

This is the entrance to the Party Pit, a jump that is (X distance?) from end to end over a row of wrecked cars and debris. Riders must make a successful **Action Check +3** to make it onto the track and take the jump. Should they succeed upon landing, the flagman will wave a checkered flag, setting off the pyro and popping the crowd. This pop will grant all members of the driver's team a -1 bonus for their next **Action Check**. When the smoke clears, a drone flies over the daredevil and drops a "prize" onto their vehicle.

Should they fail, they crash and must roll a d10 to determine where they end up. Their vehicle will take 10 LP damage, **2 Guts Penalties**, and any additional damage or penalties related to the area they end up in when they crash. The crowd will also start throwing garbage onto the course resulting in a -1 penalty for all members of the driver's team's next **Action Checks**.

Party Fail" Vehicle Placement: 1-5 North East Section / 6-10 South East Section

GR Notes: The drone dropped "prize" will come in the form of a weapon or power up for the vehicle. See chart below. Prizes may only be awarded to the Hellsings.

Party Pit Prizes

1) Flash Grenade
2) Hand Grenade
3) 5 LP Morbius Brick
4) 10 LP Morbius Brick
5) 15 LP Morbius Brick
6) Nitro Boost
7) Nitrus Boost II
8) Nitrus Boost III
9) Rocket Launcher
10) Smoke Bombs

Combat Stage 1: Monster Mash - Hellsings vs. Monster Trucks.

Combat Stage 2: You can skip this stage if the players agreed to battle the Slaughter Sisters. If the players did not agree to the battle then the Man in the Silver Suit says, "Well, this is getting a little boring! Let's send in the clowns!"

Clowns on Bikes - Apocalypse "Rodeo-style" clowns on dirtbikes enter the course to wreak havoc. Their stats are the same as Dweebs on Bike. One per every two players.

Once a monster truck is destroyed, or they all reach half their luck points, read the following:

> The Man in the Silver Suit holds a book in his left hand and recites into his microphone, "Here is a quote from the late great Edgar Allen Poe. Ahem. What good is a pit without a fucking pendulum!?"
>
> A large double-bladed pendulum descends from the ceiling and begins to swing.

Combat Stage 3: The Party Pit and the Pendulum. - A large double-sided pendulum descends from the ceiling and swings back and forth across the Party Pit and over the north and south sides of the track. It looks sharp as hell and is an unwelcome new roadblock to deal with.

> Before you can finish the Murder Hearse, Borgir says, "Borgir knows when they are beaten!"
>
> They pull off the heavy iron chains that held them fast to the casket, abandoning their Gore Gun and jumping to the ground.
>
> Even though their silver and black corpse paint is now a crackled mess, Borgir still towers over all of you. They are easily heard over the awed silence of the crowd. "Here are my keys. You may take your friend."
>
> Borgir walks back through the entrance but not before stopping to add, "It was a good battle."
>
> The crowd roars to life! The Man in the Silver Suit yells over the cheers, "Bravo! What a show! The winners of tonight's battle, the Hellsings! Take what's yours!" He claps his hands, and the cage holding Cub slowly descends.

Murder Hearse

17ft Length, 13ft Width, 11ft Height, 12,000 lbs., 2 Riders

Description:As the leader of the Slaughter Sisters, Borgir got the first pick of the vehicles left behind at the ReSolv Center and for her, it was a no-brainer. Dr. Coffin's Last Ride was a fan favorite of horror heads and regular fans with its eerie smoke show and rising casket becoming a staple of the Monster's Ball. For Borgir, it represented a way to strike terror into her foes, acting as a visual representation of their ultimate fate when facing the Slaughters Sisters. Adding to the sinister imagery,

75 LP
Action 5
Brains
Brawn 8
Cool
Charm
Guts 8

Borgir fitted the Murder Hearse with a cannon that shot projectiles made up of her victim's body parts, an ammunition type that is not in short supply these days.

1 Attack or 1 SA

Raining Blood (And Mud): The Murder Hearse will do a doughnut in the mud and spit mud from its tires and human blood from its tailpipe. This action will create a road hazard and cause all vehicles in a 30ft radius to take a +1 penalty to their next **Action Check.**

Gore Gun: DMG 0 In the cargo bed of the Murder Hearse sits an open casket with a massive cannon attached to it. This cannon fires the chopped-up human remains of the Slaughter Sister's victims straight from Borgir's abattoir. In addition to damage, any vehicle hit by the cannon's carnage must make a **Cool Check** at a +1 penalty or lose their lunch and take a +2 penalty to their next **Action Check.**

Special Ability - Metal Meltdown: DMG +2 The Gore Gun's secondary ammunition is a corrosive acid that will melt through even the toughest steel. In addition to damage, any vehicle hit by this acid will also receive a **Guts Penalty** and a +2 penalty to their next **Action Check.**

GR Notes: Should a player or enemy combatant be outside of their vehicle and struck by the acid, the damage will be +5, and they will instantly incur 2 Guts Penalties.

Special Ability - Buried Alive: DMG +3 The Murder Hearse will purposefully ram itself into another vehicle its size or smaller, attempting to run it off the road or into a road hazard, causing LP damage to their opponent and forcing them to make a **Guts Check** or suffer **1 Guts Penalty.** To avoid sliding into a hazard, the driver must make a **Brawn Check +3** to maintain control of their vehicle or slide off the road, taking additional environmental damage.

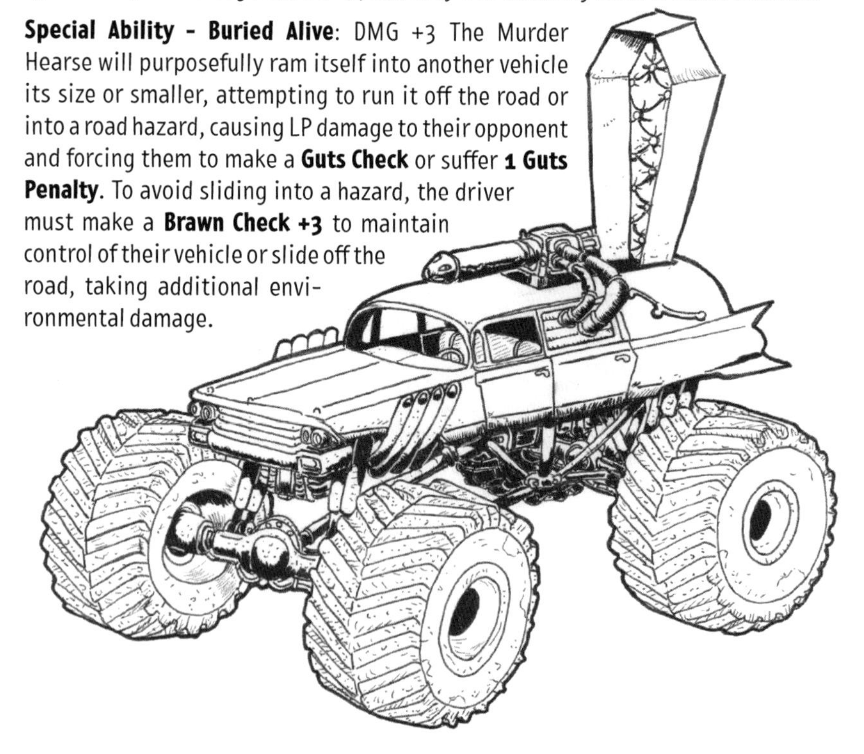

The Blasphemizer

17ft Length, 13ft Width, 11ft Height, 12,000 lbs., 2 Riders

Description:Of the many monster trucks left behind when the ReSolv Center was evacuated halfway through the Monster's Ball, Sister Christian was the one Tuuala, a lifelong heavy metal fan, hated the most. This holy roller was originally intended to inspire awe with its church organ piped exhaust and a new Biblical verse painted on its hood every Sunday. After seeing how repulsed Tuula was by it, Borgir gave it to her as a joke. Tuuala saw it as a challenge instead. She disappeared into the Sister's garage for six days, blasting nothing but King Diamond. On the seventh day, she emerged and rested, having perverted the one-time champion of faith into a servant of the dark lord, the Blasphemizer.

75 LP

Action 5
Brains
Brawn 8
Cool
Charm
Guts 8

1 Attack or 1 SA

Unholy Roller: DMG 0 The Blasphenizer will rear and then drive over any smaller vehicle or multiple vehicles within a 10-foot sphere, resulting in damage and **1 Guts Penalty**.

Shout At The Devil: DMG -5 This sonic boom attack will hit all vehicles in its path resulting in damage and **1 Guts Penalty**.

Special Ability - Caught In A Mosh: DMG +3 The Blasphemizer will purposefully ram itself into another vehicle its size or smaller, attempting to run it off the road or into a road hazard, causing LP damage to their opponent and forcing them to make a **Guts Check** or suffer **1 Guts Penalty**. To avoid sliding into a hazard, the driver must make a **Brawn Check +3** to maintain control of their vehicle or slide off the road, taking additional environmental damage.

Special Ability - Upsidedown Cross: **Devil Horn Gun**s - DMG +5 / **Weight of the Cross** DMG +20 If the Blasphemizer is near any crushed vehicles, embankments, or ramps, it may make an Action Check +3 to attempt a backflip assault against its foes.

If successful, the Blasphemizer will shoot its opponents with the Devil Horn Guns while upside down during the flip and then crush its opponent with the Weight of the Cross on their landing. If their opponent is not destroyed, they will receive 3 **Guts Penalties**.

Should the Blasphemizer fail, however, it will miss with the guns and crash upside down upon landing. This will result in DMG +10, 2 **Guts Penalties**, the Devil Horn Guns becoming unusable, and a lost turn. During that lost turn, the Blasphemizer must make a successful **Action Check +3** to flip over or lose another turn.

GR Notes: While overturned, the Blasphemizer is susceptible to damage. All attacks against it will receive +3 damage. Should a player want to commandeer Blasphemizer while in this state, a straight **Action Check** will suffice.

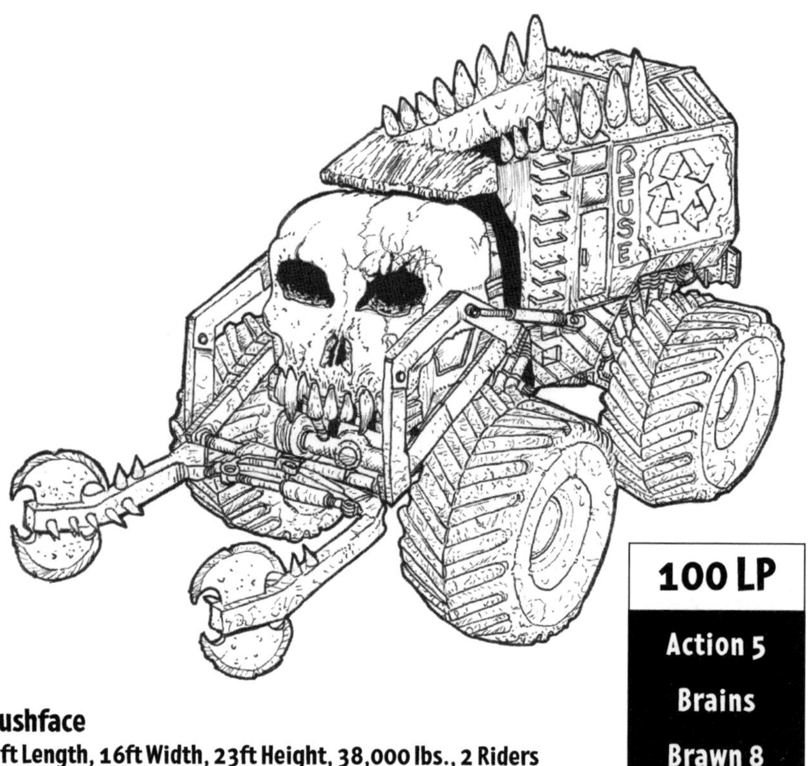

100 LP
Action 5
Brains
Brawn 8
Cool
Charm
Guts 8

Crushface

27ft Length, 16ft Width, 23ft Height, 38,000 lbs., 2 Riders

Description: Azraph found herself drawn to the Monster Truck Crush because it reminded her of her late mother, the Chairwoman of the local Trash Collection Union in Topeka. When she joined the Slaughter Sisters, she swore it would one day be hers.

1 Attack or 1 SA

Axe: DMG 0 This Pick Axe style front loaders slash and make ready their target for extraction. In addition to damage, the players must make a successful **Guts Check +1** for their vehicles or suffer 1 **Guts Penalty**.

Smash: DMG +5 This ramming attack will happen at the rear of the enemy vehicle with Crushface attempting to drive over its foe with the front wheels only. In addition to damage, the players must make a successful **Guts Check +1** for their vehicles or suffer 2 **Guts Penalties**.

Special Ability - Crush: if Crushface can make a successful **Action Check +3** it may use its front loader to pick up an enemy vehicle and drop it into its garbage compactor. The players will have an opportunity to make a **Brawn Check +3** to attempt to break their vehicle free before they are lifted into the compactor. If they fail, they take DMG +20 plus 3 **Guts Penalties**.

GR Notes: If a player's vehicle gets wasted in the compactor, Crushface must take a full turn to dump it out onto the track before making another attack.

It must remain still while dumping the crushed remains and thus becomes susceptible to damage. Any attacks against Crushface while emptying its compactor will be at a +3 to damage.

If the players attempt to commandeer Crushface at this point they will receive a -1 bonus to their **Action Check**. If it's the player whose vehicle was wasted in the compactor, they will get a -2 bonus to their attempt to commandeer.

Special Ability - RAM: DMG +3 Crushface will purposefully ram itself into another vehicle its own size or smaller, attempting to run it off the road or into a road hazard, causing LP damage to their opponent and forcing them to make a **Guts Check** or suffer 1 **Guts Penalty**. To avoid sliding into a hazard, the driver must make a **Brawn Check +3** to maintain control of their vehicle or slide off the road, taking additional environmental damage.

End Of The Episode Wrap-Up And Awards Ceremony

As you wrap for the night or for a quick break before the next episode, have the players roll 1d10 to replenish Luck Points. They may always re-roll a 1. Remember, there is **no maximum for Luck Points**. You can also do an **End of the Episode Award Ceremony**, letting the group vote, giving out awards for:

Best Action Sequence: +1 Luck Points

Best Commandeering: +2 Luck Points

Best Joke or One Liner: +3 Luck Points

Best Kill: +4 Luck Points

Episode 4: Goodbye Yellow Brick Road

Scene 1: Return of KeyLow

Cub runs up to Bear and wraps his arms around her. She pushes him back and slaps him on the back of the head before she grabs him tight and whispers, "I'm so sorry."

Bear notices everyone gathered around and composes herself, saying "Just please don't go all reckless again, Cub, okay?"

"Okay," he agrees.

The Silo stands tall against the orange and purple dusk that slowly overtook the day. Everyone eased into the calm night, the pride of a job well done settling in against the warm feeling of being a complete gang once more. As you relax, you see a familiar face walking up the road. It vaguely looks like Keylow, although more machine now than scumbag.

"I come in peace. I just need to talk," his voice was a breathless synthetic crackle. "There's something you need to know."

Croc takes a step forward and holds up his knife, "Now, Keylow, you still kind of alive? Last I heard, some of my crew here gave you a bad day."

Croc turns back to you all and gives a cautious nod, "Let's hear what you have to say. But if you are doing something shady, I'll gut those servos and not think twice about it. Hell, I might even do it anyway after hearing what you have to say."

"Get in line. Scorp put a bounty on my head 'cause he thinks I killed the Naa Zaa or got him killed. Either way, he ain't too happy with me. So I got nothing to lose right now. I just thought you'd want you to know that Boar is still alive, for the moment at least. Death Point Raiders want to make a show of killing him. They're sending a message. They want to warn all the other bands to stay away while they make their play against the Black Swans."

"A bounty sounds right. Scorp ain't exactly the forgiving kind," Croc says. "Why should we believe you?"

"While I was getting fixed up, the chop shop guy, a real weirdo named Comfort Eagle, told me Death Point was planning a parade. They'll be driving Boar down the RT 71 highway tomorrow at noon. I know which way they are coming and I know how many people they will have. I know it all," Keylow says. "Death Point is planning a war, Croc. I don't do wars. I'll trade you the info for a ride. I'm going to head to the coast after tonight. Consider me retired. This whole place is literally about to explode."

Croc put his knife away.

"Alright, let's hear what you got."

GR Notes: Let the players know that the next battle will be tough and long. Players can use any previously acquired ride for this particular mission and a pool of 20 additional Luck Points can be divided up amongst their rides.

Scene 2: Boar's Gauntlet

The steel caravan blazed down the highway leaving a mighty dragon tail of dust in its wake. The sun had become a hazy golden disc in the sky, fighting to be seen through the omnipresent dust. Suspended high above on the back of a truck fabricated to resemble his codename, Boar pulled at the bonds holding his arms apart as clouds circled him like a water going down a drain.

"Listen up, even though it might be a triple-double cross, we gotta take a chance to rescue Boar. Just like we'd take a chance to rescue any of you," Croc's voice crackled as the metallic dust interfered with the helmet's signal. "We take the head. You take the tail. We meet in the middle."

Crocs' Trans Am cut across the fallow field on the opposite side of the highway. Fox and Cub followed in a Dune Buggy and Hawk in a gyrocopter above.

"Scorp is smart so he'll be expecting us and I'm sure he'll have some surprises planned, so keep your wits about you and an eye peeled for anything crazy."

You pull onto the highway and see four Dweebs on bikes, 15-foot Death Point Raider banners streaming in the wind behind them.

This is a full-on high-speed parade, the beginning set piece for another multi-stage battle where the Hellsings try to save Boar and the Death Point Raiders are out for payback. This combat will also lead to a major plot point in the story. The Hellsings should be pushed to the limit before this module ends.

Combat Stage 1: The Death Point Raider's opening salvo comes in the form of four Dweebs on motorcycles with front and rear-facing machine guns. They will attempt to stay out of melee range and work to soften up the Hellsings and cause a distraction from their oncoming air support.

GR Notes: Halfway through the combat there is a great opportunity to ratchet up the tension by hinting at something coming in the distance but obscured by the dust and clouds.

When the last Dweeb is down to half their LP, they will wave their flag from the pole in the back of the bike. This will signal their air support which will arrive in combat on the next turn.

A red light illuminates the clouds of dust behind you. A Dweeb in a gyrocopter burst out of the clouds flanked by flying attack drones. Each drone is approximately five feet in size with four top-mounted propeller blades. A laser-guided gun barrel and bombs are also attached to each unit.

Combat Stage 2: The Dweeb-O-Copter cuts through the clouds and always attacks the Hellsings flying vehicles before attacking any ground vehicles. The drones will attempt to swarm the vehicles and act as a deadly nuisance.

GR Notes: The number of drones in combat should be determined by the number of players and scaled accordingly. They are meant to beat up but not outright defeat the players before the next combat stage.

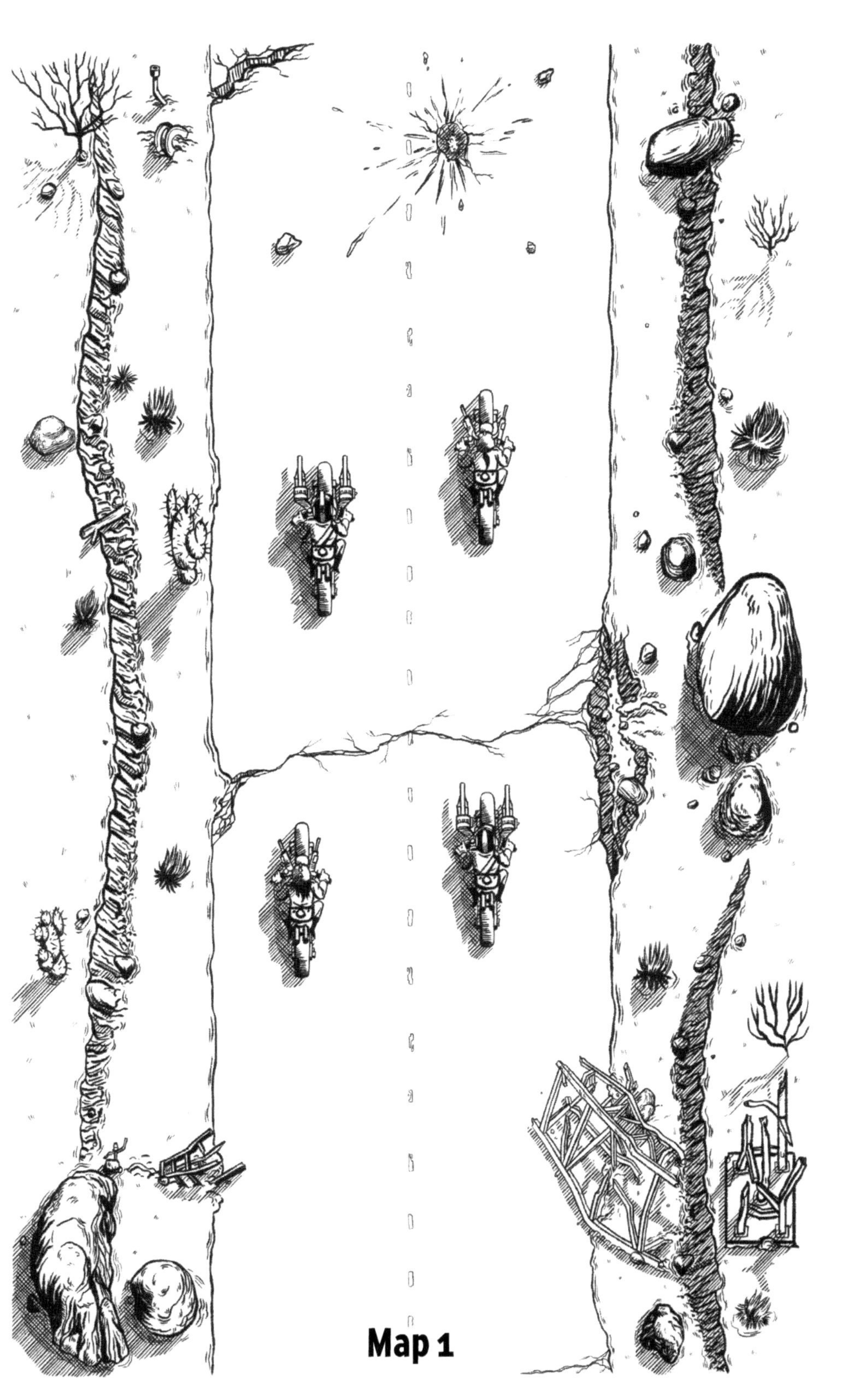

Map 1

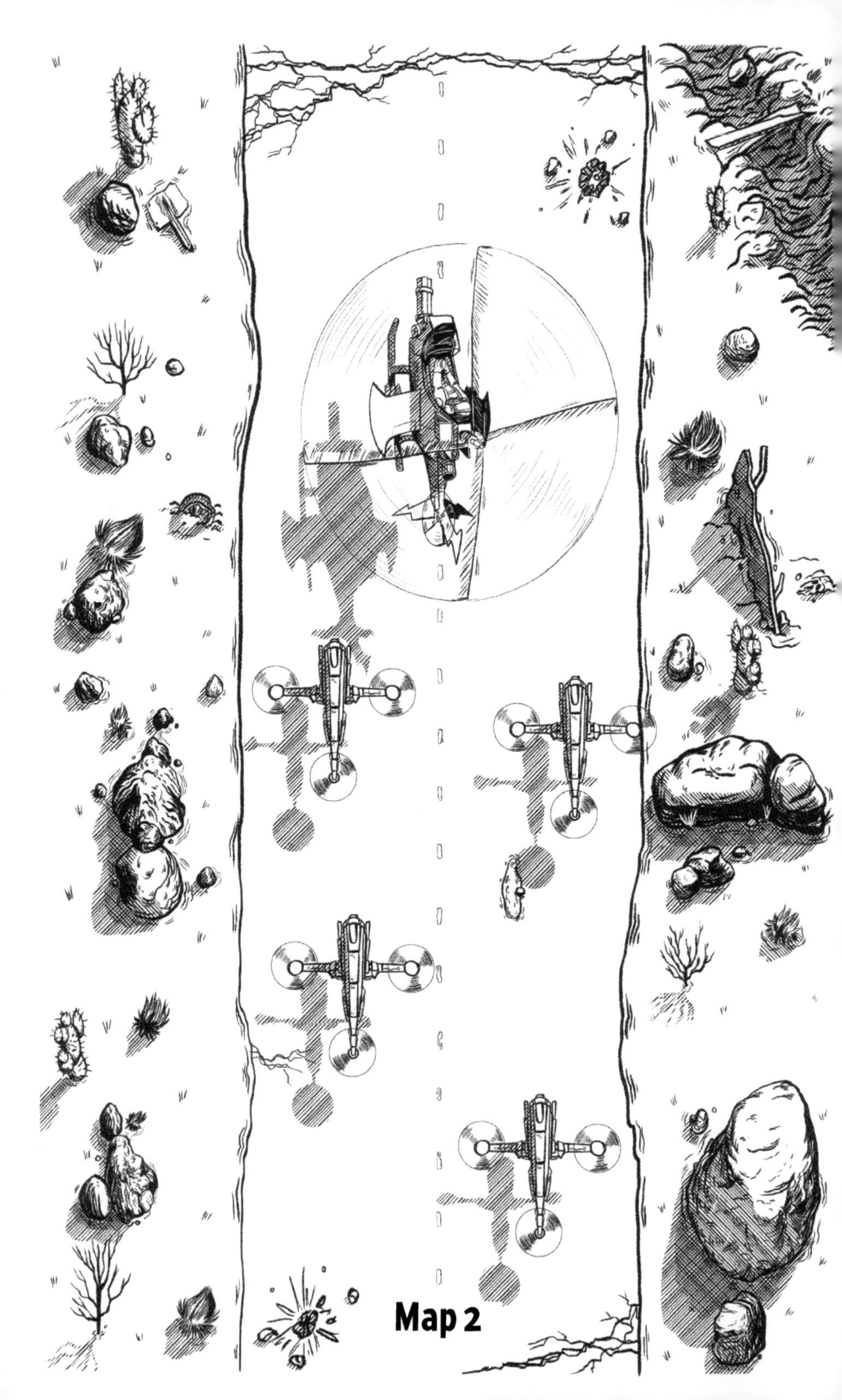
Map 2

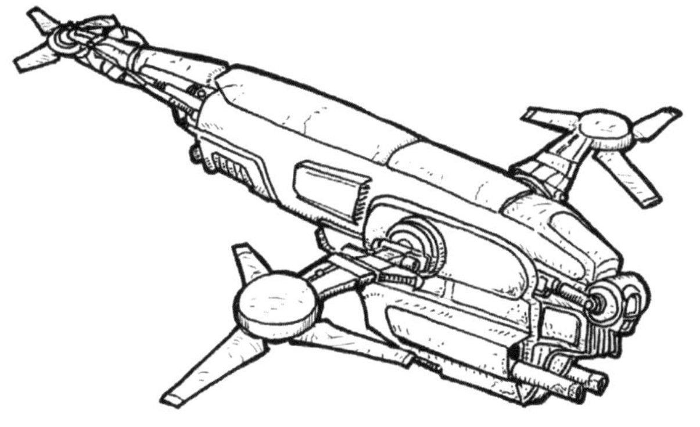

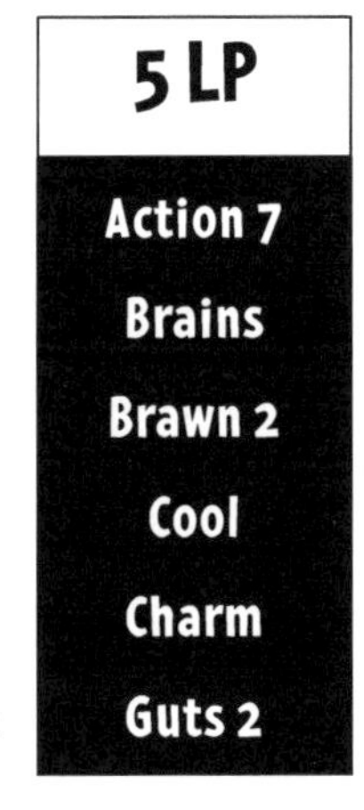

"The Spy" Van Zandt VZ-76 V2.

Surveillance Drones (Battery Powered) - 4ft Length, 4ft Width, 1ft Height, 30lbs.

Description:The VZ-76 Surveillance drones were initially designed by Van Zandt Technologies as a home security drone for their consumer sales division. With the blossoming of an ongoing partnership between the US military and Van Zandt, this was yet another creation repurposed to suit the military's needs. The V2. version was expanded in size, battery power and lethality with the addition of a small caliber "Pea Shooter" minigun.

1 Attack

Pea Shooter: 30 Round Magazzine, DMG -7

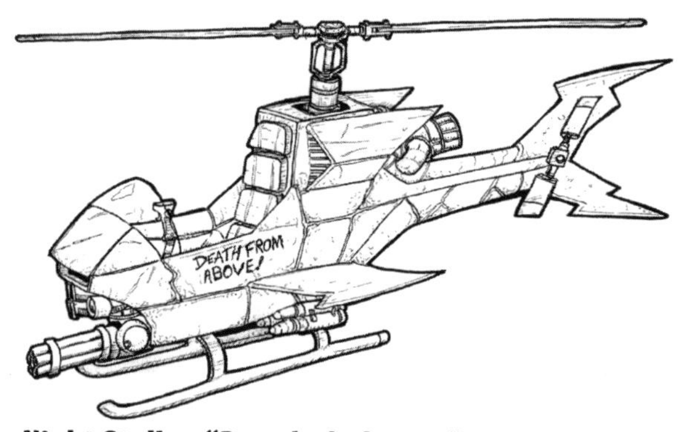

25 LP
Action 7
Brains
Brawn 3
Cool
Charm
Guts 4

The Night Stalker "Dweeb-O-Copter"
(Carbon Plus Powered) - 16 ft Length, 6ft Width, 9ft Height, 584lbs., One Rider/One Hanger On

Description: The Night Stalker, a single-passenger Carbon+ powered helicopter, was a fan favorite during the early days of the Amphikura War. It earned its moniker due to its Tanzeer designed "Quiet Motor" and Van Zandt "Whispering Rotor". When you add in its "Starry Night" colorway, the Night Stalker became practically invisible, which made it ideal for discretely maneuvering in and out of hot spots.

2 Attacks or 1 SA Per Turn

Front Mounted Machine Gun: 50 Round Drum Magazine, DMG -2

Special Ability - Manic Missiles!: 6 Missiles, DMG -3/0/+3 The Dweeb-O-Copter has two missile racks with three missiles each that may be fired, one rack per turn at multiple or a single target. Each missile has an individual DMG of -3 if fired at an individual target, but if combined against a single target will scale to 0 for two missiles or +3 for three missiles when used together.

Special Ability - "Get The Net": (One Use Only) The Dweeb-O-Copter has a 500lb weighted net that it can drop on an unsuspecting vehicle, car-sized or smaller. The pilot must make an **Action Check +3** to drop it accurately and if it catches its prey, a car-sized vehicle will take a +2 penalty to **Action Checks** and a motorcycle-sized vehicle will be immediately incapacitated for one turn. The target's opponents will be granted a +2 bonus to their damage while the net is in play.

Once the Dweeb-O-Copter is defeated, read the following:

Croc comes through on your headset and says, "We're pinned down. They got air support. Take out their broadcast truck!"

You spot a truck with a dish and antenna on top; drones stream out of its sides like fighter jets. It has to be the broadcast truck. Before you can make your way toward it, a frankensteined armored truck with a full-sized tank turret on it charges at you from the side of the highway.

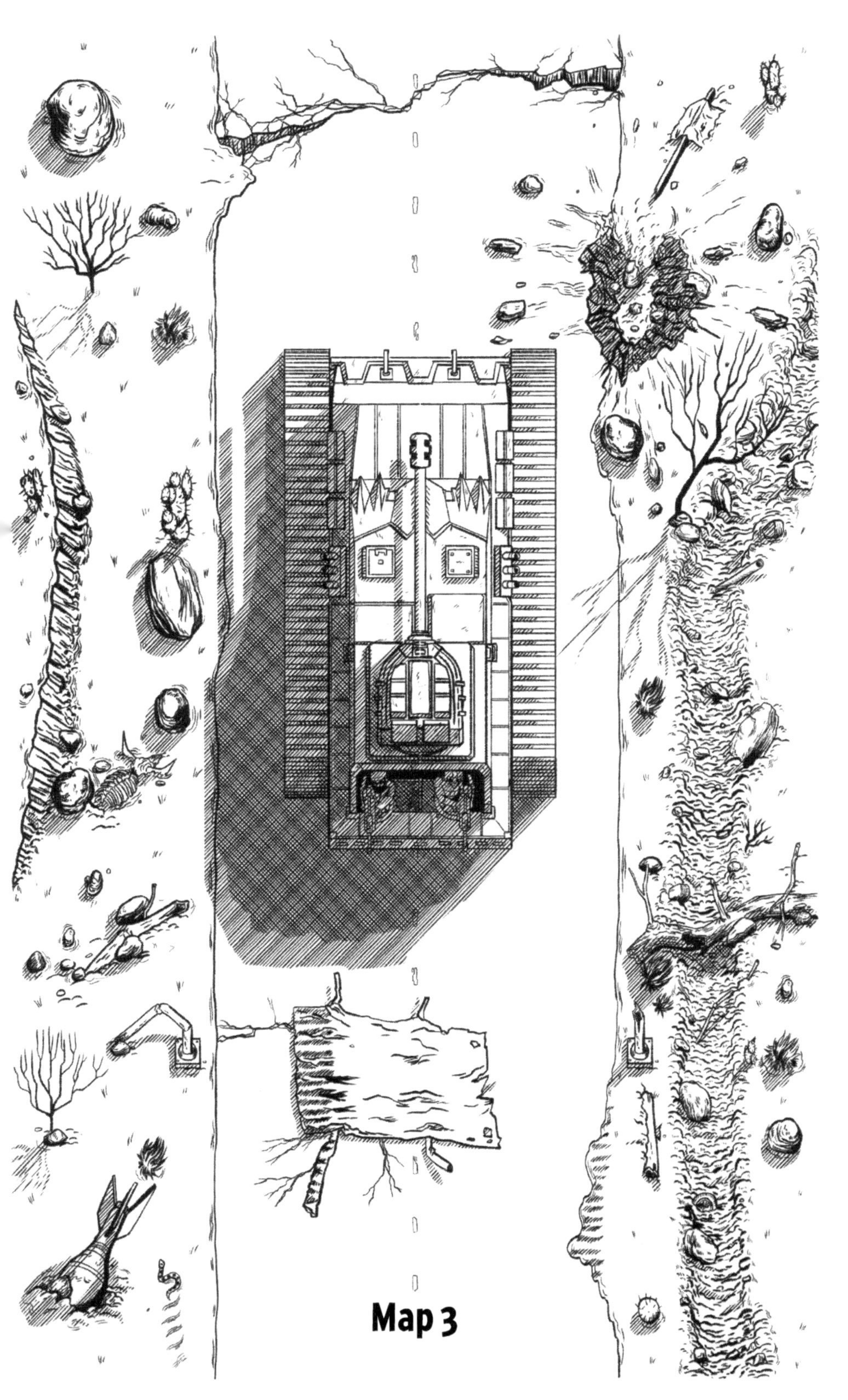
Map 3

Combat Stage 3: After the Hellsings break free of the air support line through the dust clouds, they will encounter the awful Tank Truck!

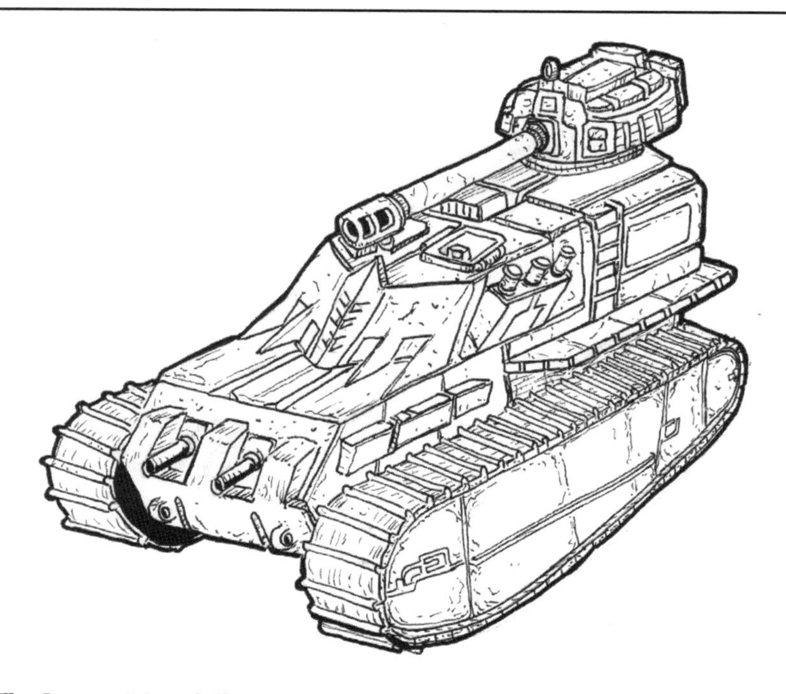

"The Reaper" Death Tank

15ft Length, 8ft Width, 10ft Height, 20,000 lbs., 1 Riders, 2 Hangar Ons

Description: An early prototype of a lightweight, fully armored tank that runs on Carbon +, the "Archie III" was a smash hit for the US military. Designed by Huxley Tanzeer and named after his late rottweiler, Archibald Tanzeer II, this tank combined an exciting new fuel source with the latest scientific weaponry. Originally assembled in a factory outside of Abeline, Texas, seven were left behind at Fort Dillion for system upgrades. Five were immediately wrecked by the Death Point Raiders, thus making the Death Tank a hot commodity in the wasteland.

100 LP
Action 7
Brains
Brawn 9
Cool
Charm
Guts 9

2 Attacks

30 Caliber Machine Gun: 200 Rounds, DMG 0 LP

Special Ability - "Good Ole' Archie" 105mm Gun: 6 Rounds, DMG +2 These large caliber rounds are specifically designed to pierce the armor of their enemies vehicles and will result in an automatic **2 Guts Penalties** in addition to damage.

GR Notes: The Death Point Raiders know this is one of their most powerful vehicles and don't trot it out often. Two Muscle Dweebs with sub-machine guns will hang near the back of the Death Tank as insurance to ensure no other gang can attempt to commandeer it.

Read the following once the Death Tank drops below half its Luck Points:

> Croc's Trans Am crosses the highway followed by a swarm of Drones. He tosses a grenade out of his window before gunning it back up the road. The grenade lands on the Death Tank and blasts the side doors wide open.

Two Dweebs mechanics on bikes ride up and jump onto the Death Tank. They start trying to fix the vehicle, repairing **1d10 Luck Points** per turn. They are in cover of the vehicle so the only way to directly damage them is to attempt to commandeer the Death Tank or completely deplete its Luck Points.

Read the following once the players commandeer or waste the Tank Tuck:

> Nothing stands between you and the broadcast truck. Hawk unloads on it from his gyrocopter before five drones chase him away. The other side opens and five more drones come flying out at you like bats out of hell.

"The Anchorman" Broadcast Truck

72ft Length, 15ft Width, 14ft Height, 30,000 lbs., Two Riders

Description: After the success of the Van Zandt surveillance drones, the military began looking for mobile options for short-range deployment. Rex Tanzeer, trying to break back into the automobile industry and encroach upon Van Zandt's new military contracts, offered a joint partnership to build a new state-of-the-art mobile communications hub using both companies' technology, dubbed "The Anchorman." While the final product is considered the finest in communications technology, the Anchorman's production was tumultuous and hindered by ego and spite, causing massive delays and ultimately starting a blood feud between the two companies.

50 LP

Action 5
Brains
Brawn 7
Cool
Charm
Guts 7

2 Attacks

Attack Drones: 10 Drones The Broadcast Truck uses Attack Drones as its main resource in combat and may dispatch two every turn to attack its foes after the initial five drones have been wasted.

Special Ability - Shock Me!: 6 Rounds, DMG +2 This massive electric cannon is mounted to the roof of the Anchorman as part of the satellite dish and will fire a blast every other turn. It needs time to recharge after an attack. In addition to damage, the target must make a **Guts Check** or suffer **1 Guts Penalty**.

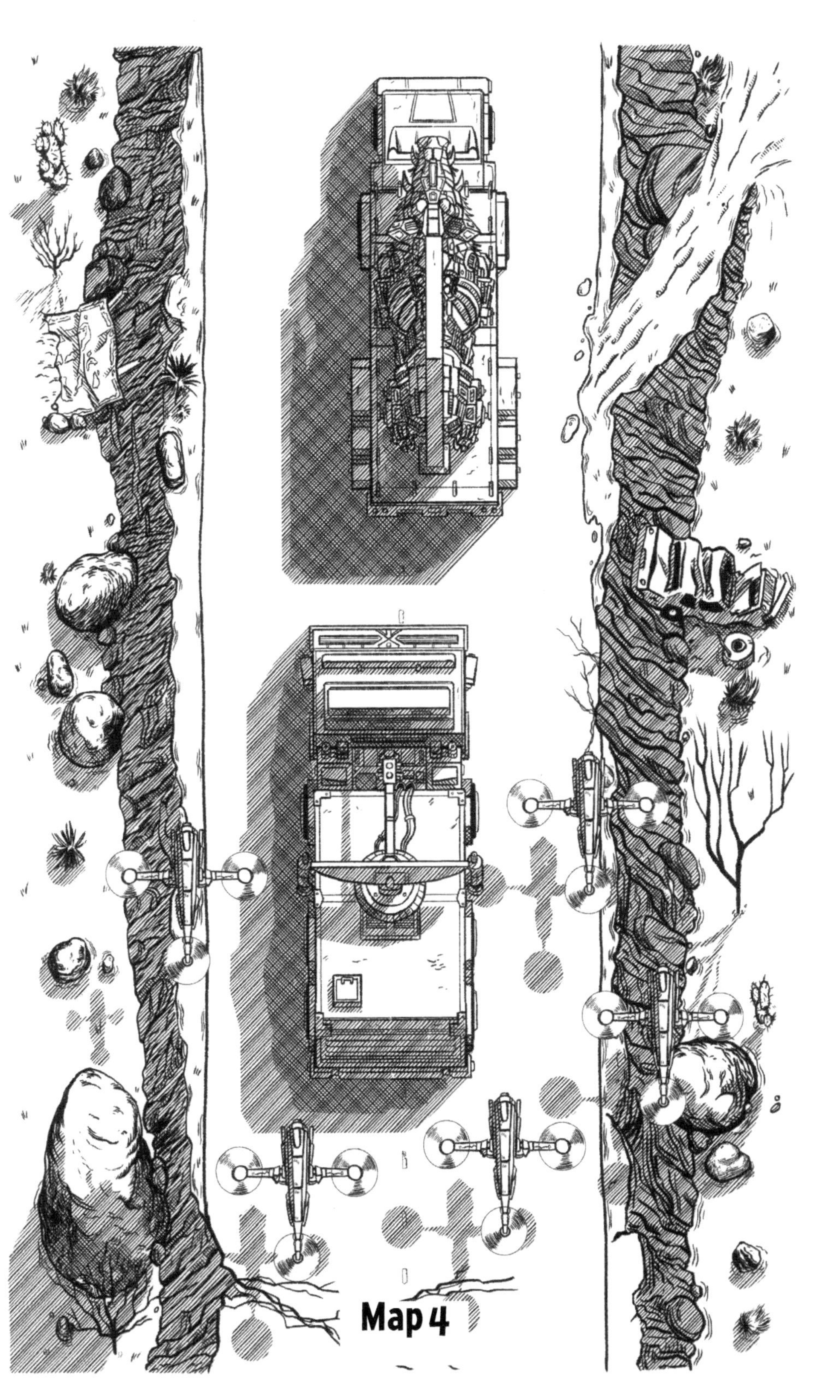
Map 4

Combat Stage 4: The Broadcast Truck is the source of the drones and will release five more drones into combat upon arrival. The drones will continue in the attack pattern established in Combat Stage 2.

GR Notes: If the players can commandeer this vehicle, they can directly attack the two dishes, each one with 15 Luck Points, and once destroyed it will deactivate all drones. If the players outright waste the Broadcast Truck, then it will destroy all drones on board and deactivate any active flying drones.

Should a player commandeer the Broadcast Truck and want to take control of the drones, they must make a successful **Brains Check +3**. Should they fail, they will be unable to take control of the drones and any active drones will do double damage to the Hellsings they are attacking.

After the Broadcast Truck is defeated, read the following:

> Boar sits in a cage 25 feet above the welded steel boar effigy. Three snipers calmly aim at the passing vehicles on the flatbed below.
>
> You watch Cub jump onto the flatbed and fight a sniper hand to hand. The other snipers drop their guns and rush to attack Cub with blades drawn.

"The Warden" Prison Truck

72ft Length, 15ft Width, 14ft Height, 20,000 lbs., Two Riders, 5 Snipers

Description: This 2052 Atlas W-Class prison transport vehicle won the top prize at the United States Police Benevolence Society's Blue Line Awards Ceremony, taking home the LaFours for excellence in Policing Implements three years running. This model ran out of fuel on Route 31 on a run from Chicago to Denver on a hot August day in 2056 and was subsequently surrounded. Originally touted by its designers to be unhijackable by force, all it took for the Death

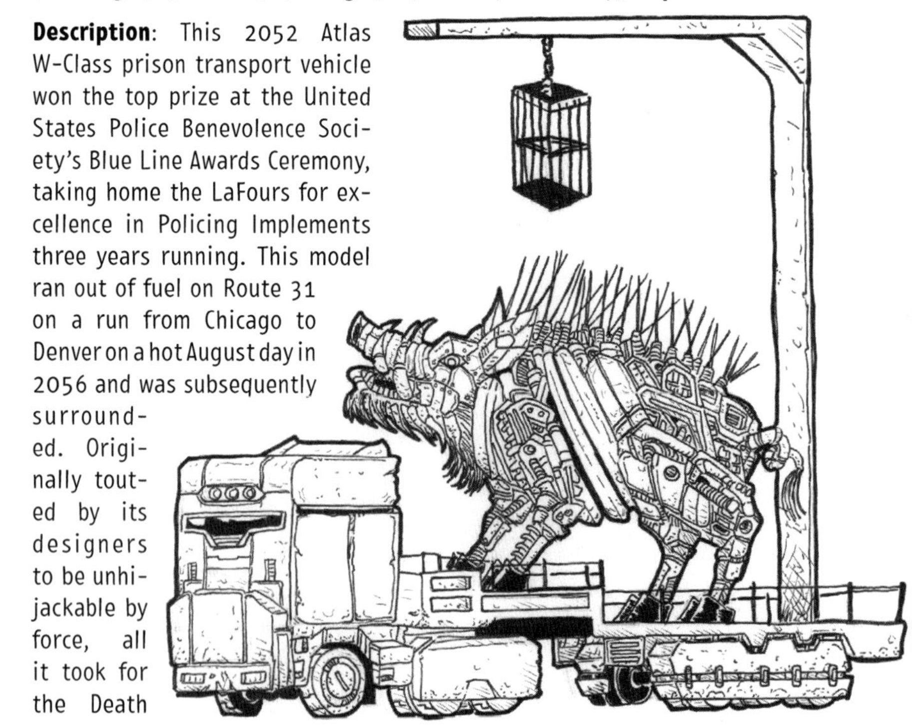

Point Raiders to claim ownership was providing some ice cold Sluice to a very dehydrated driver.

1 Attack

Black Betty: DMG +5 The Warden will purposefully ram itself into another vehicle its size or smaller, attempting to run it off the road or into a road hazard causing LP damage to their opponent and forcing them to make a **Guts Check** or suffer **2 Guts Penalties**. To avoid sliding into a hazard, the driver must make a **Brawn Check +3** to maintain control of their vehicle or slide off the road, taking additional environmental damage.

50 LP

Action 7

Brains

Brawn 9

Cool

Charm

Guts 9

Combat Stage 5: The snipers will attempt to pick off the Hellsings to provide cover and time to allow the Dweebs on ATVs to enter combat.

The ATV Dweebs will do their best to prevent the Hellsings from getting within striking range of the Prison Truck. Should one of them break through and attempt to commandeer the Prison truck one sniper will remain shooting at the other Hellsings while the rest enter combat. If only one Sniper remains and a commandeering occurs, they will abandon their post and attack the player directly.

Should the Truck still be under enemy control, a player must make a **Brains Check +2** or a **Brawn Check +2** to free Boar. Failure will result in them being launched off the truck unless they can make an **Action Check +3**. If they fail their **Action Check**, they will hit the road and take **10 Luck Point** Damage and **1 Guts Penalty**.

If the Broadcast Truck is commandeered, Boar may be freed without a Check being made.

1968 Pontiac LeMans

(Carbon Powered) 17ft Length, 9ft Width, 4ft Height, 3,287 lbs., Two Riders

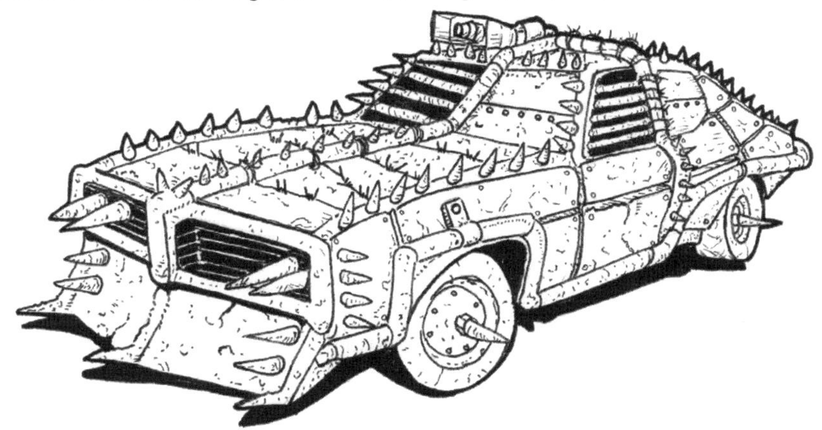

30 LP
Action 7
Brains
Brawn 8
Cool
Charm
Guts 8

Description:This former four-door gas guzzler once belonged to Scorp's great grandfather and has since been converted to full Carbon+. Built for battering and blocking, the LeMans front end is equipped with a spike-lined cow pusher and its trunk hood and roof are lined with various bits of barbed wire and jagged spikes for maximum discomfort. The rear and driver-side passenger doors have also been welded shut to prevent enemy commandeering, leaving the only entry point the driver's side window.

1 Attack + 1 SA Per Turn

Car Ram-Rod: DMG +2 The LeMans will purposefully ram itself into another vehicle attempting to run it off the road causing LP damage to their opponent's vehicle and forcing them to make a **Guts Check+1** or suffer 1 **Guts Penalty**.

Special Ability - "The Malachi Crunch!": DMG 0 This legendary maneuver, perfected in the 1950s by the maniacal Malachi Brothers, typically takes a willing partner but can also be done as long as its victim ends up sandwiched between two vehicles. The LaMans will ram either its front or rear bumper into an opponent, slamming it into a teammate's vehicle (with the teammate also doing the same) or any vehicle on the other side of their opponent. In addition to damage, the opponent must make a **Guts Check +2** or take 1 **Guts Penalty**, and the vehicle on the other side of the crunch will take half damage and must make a **Guts Check +1** or suffer a **Guts Penalty**.

Scene 3: We don't need another Hero

Once Boar is free, read the following:

You hear a horn blaring in the distance as you free Boar. Another Death Point Raider convoy is coming up the highway with at least 15 more vehicles.

A Gold Pontiac Le Man that looks like it's ready for war pulls up next to you. Over its loudspeaker Scorp says, "This is enough. It's time to stop these small squabbles. All we do is deplete each other's resources so the masters can continue to run roughshod over the plains. Croc, I challenge you! Me versus you, my wheels against yours. We end this right now and no one else dies. "

The dust crackles like an old record waiting for its first song.

"One thing I could always count on was you all doing something unexpected. I could hold that tight and close and feel secure that I chose each of you for the right reasons. You are all wild animals and I'm so proud. But I'm also tired. I'm tired of Hellsings getting wasted for no reason in this feud. This wasn't the reason I started this band. It's my turn to do something reckless..."

"Scorp, let's do this!" Croc says over his car loudspeaker.

Croc and Scorp peel out and drive to opposing ends of the highway then whip around and stop.

The thrum of the convoy is the only sound in the air until Croc presses play on his tape deck. A song wails to life, breaking the silence, and they both start to tear down the road. They aim at each other at full speed. Croc is blasting The Hellsings at full volume from his Trans Am. Scorp's Pontiac is deadly quiet.

They collide like a star imploding. Both cars shear through one another and the Pontiac spins then turns end over end. The Trans Am flips in the air before landing on its back. Death Point Raiders rush to pull Scorp from the car. He's unconscious and covered in blood.

Croc's Trans Am lays upside down, faintly smoking, as fire begins to lick up the crushed hood. You run towards it but are brought to your knees as the car explodes into a white-hot fireball.

You never see Croc again.

End Of The Episode Wrap Up And Awards Ceremony

As you wrap for the night or for a quick break before the next episode, have the players roll 1d10 to replenish Luck Points. They may always re-roll a 1. Remember, there is no maximum for Luck Points. You can also do an **End of the Episode Award Ceremony**, letting the group vote, giving out awards for:

Best Action Sequence: +1 Luck Points

Best Commandeering: +2 Luck Points

Best Joke or One Liner: +3 Luck Points

Best Kill: +4 Luck Points

Catch you next time!

Episode 5: Carry on Wayward Son

It's quiet at the Silo over the next few days. Everybody goes about their business as well as they can. There is grief thick in the air. It's pervasive and drips like a tightly rung rag over every Hellsing. The grief never stops, but dishes still have to be washed and vehicles fixed.

Bear and Cub work in the garage every morning, Bee teaches the orphans, and Crow and Fox go on scouting missions to update maps and ledgers. Boar's been drinking; the guilt has been particularly rough on him. No other bands have even made a peep, giving you all a sense of morbid peace.

One morning you see Bee hesitating and talking to himself. He looks over at you as if he's made a decision before walking up to where you're standing. He hands you an original pressing vinyl of Sunset City Blood Driver, The Hellsing's first full-length album and considered by some to be their best.

"Croc put me in charge of some of his things if anything ever happened. He'd want you to have this. It was one of his prized possessions. There's also a note inside."

The note reads:

"Well, if you got this, I'm dead 'cause I said the only way anybody would ever be able to take this from me was from my cold dead hands. It's weird being dead, or at least writing from the death side of things. I had a fun life and always had a good time. It was crazy. I have regrets, but I guess that's necessary 'cause it means you know where you started. I should have gone to Kansas City Sounds again. It's the Hellsing mecca for more reasons than one. If a Hellsing reads this, go to Kansas City Sounds pronto. If you're not a Hellsing, put this album on and become one."

You carefully open the gatefold cover and see black and white pictures from an old world that no longer exists. They look almost medieval. A bunch of kids surrounded by wires and equipment laughing. Guitars and microphones are all arranged to look super cool. And, in the corner, there is an address for the studio.

The players can do a few things before going to Kansas City Sounds. If they talk to Bee, he is pretty adamant about the players going. He'll say things like, "You guys better not waste too much time 'cause you never know how much you have left." and "It's what Croc would have wanted."

Bear and **Cub** got all the vehicles in decent shape. Everything unlocked is available to use at full luck points. The players can visit the makeshift grave at the edge of the property. The rough engraving on the cross says Godspeed Croc.

Crow and **Fox** say it's been tranquil and they have no new info on any bands making moves. They add that they do have one bit of tasty info, though. The word is Scorp survived the duel but the Death Point Raiders have shut down all their expansion operations. There's no word on his state of health.

If the player talks to **Boar**, he's tipsy but shows you what he's been working on. He'll bring you to a shed at the property's edge and pull the tarp off of Croc's Trans Am. The paint job is rough, and the body needs a little work, but he got it to run with a little help from Bear in her spare time. He offers you the keys.

The players can equip whatever cars are available to them for the next bit, investigating Kansas City Sounds.

Scene 1: Kansas City Sounds

It's your first time in the big city, though big city is a relative term. Anything is bigger than where you came from. People bustled, hustled, and filled the streets back in its heyday. These days the big city was a big graveyard, with cement buildings like tombstones and ivy lining them like unkempt wreaths. Graffiti fills every space possible. One frequent tag you see that blots out the rest is The Urchins. Their logo is a spiny, chaotic bramble. You never really heard of them; they must keep to the city like rats.

The studio is in the south end of town. It's a nondescript building with no signs, no windows, just a heavy reinforced door and a buzzer. A voice rings out over a small intercom and says, "Hellsings? Well, come on in". The buzzer chimes loudly and the door mechanism unlatches.

The door creaks open and you can hear some low-end thump deeper in the building, kick drums and bass reverberating through the walls. You follow it and the closer you get the more you can hear. Guitars start to howl in time with cymbals as vocals kick in for a Hellsings song you have never heard.

When you step into a massive control room you see something pushing the faders. It's a human sized roach with a human face. "Good morning," it says as you stare in shock. "Yeah, I know, I know, some real Kafka shit. I'm Jimmy Larouche. Drummer for The Hellsings."

Players can take a minute to let that sink in.

Scene 2: UmmaGumma

Jimmy tells you about Croc's dilemma.

"Croc left the Black Swans but never got out from under their shadow. They forced him to take the lead in an attack against the Death Point Raiders which led to losing members of his band and his home. Croc never recovered. The guilt ate him up. Resolv Corp, which I know a lot about from a lifetime ago, has been funding the Black Swans. They want chaos. Resolv wants bands squabbling because it makes it easier to control the midwest without a unified front. They blossomed in the vacuum with a field of lab rats to use for experiments. There will be no peace until Resolv or the Swans are gone from the midwest."

"There's a little something I've been working on. It's a call to arms, really. The Hellsings, the band making waves, asking everyone to attack their local Black Swans outpost. While the Black Swans are distracted, you all attack the head. You can take out the Black Swans leadership and then the Resolv Corporate headquarters."

As this plan starts to percolate in your mind, he reaches out for you.

"I have one last present for you."

Jimmy has five syringes of UMA in his clawed hand.

"These are different blends from the crud I took. They're more controlled and will enhance you and bring out your animals. Croc took the first one. It made him tougher, gave him that hard skin. He hoped to come back and get more for everyone, but... Anyway, this might give you the edge that you need!"

GR Notes: Should the players decide to inject themselves, the player's special abilities will either become enhanced or a new special ability will unlock as detailed in their character description.

Hellsings UMA Upgrades

Dog: UMA Special Ability - "And Now I'm Angry": Once per scene, Dog can decide to lose his cool and become a rage-fueled hulking brute. His **Action**, **Brawn**, and **Guts** stats all become 9, and he becomes impervious to damage for three turns. His melee strike damage is increased to +5, and he can easily tear through materials like steel. The downside is at the end of his rage break, he will endure 2 **Guts Penalties** (to a maximum of 3 **Guts Penalties**) and a +2 penalty to his **Action Checks** for two turns.

Cat: UMA Special Ability - "Punch It Squeegee": Cat can communicate telepathically with her prairie dog Squeegee and, once per scene, unlock his true form which is a 6ft tall battle beast. While Squeegee is in Beast Mode, Cat may ride him into battle or command his actions on the battlefield. While mounted, Squeegee will adhere to the vehicle battle rules as if he were a car or motorcycle, protecting Cat from any direct damage or **Guts Penalties.**

Squeegee: UMA Special Ability - Battle Squee!: When Squeegee enters his battle beast mode, he will be able to run at 60mph and on vertical surfaces. While Squeegee may be indestructible, he has a finite number of Luck Points for when he is in beast mode. Squeegee will return to normal size when those Luck Points are expended and need a nap.

Battle Squeegee

Superintelligent Pet - 6ft tall, 2,300 lbs.

30 LP
Action 8
Brains 7
Brawn 9
Cool 5
Charm 4
Guts 9

Special Ability - Snack Time!: DMG +6 While Squeegee's normal urge lean towards Cheese Puffs and potato chips, in the battle mode he becomes a lot hungrier and a lot less discriminate over what he eats. Only his friends are safe from his appetite because while he may get hangry, friends are not food. With that said, everything else is on the table.

Do You Want To Catch These Hands?: DMG -2 Squeeegee's claws become razor sharp and ready to rip through concrete, metal, and wood easily. While sharp enough to pinch when he's normal size, these mitts are now made to maul in beast mode!

Rat: UMA Special Ability - Backstab Outta Knowhere: Rat can short distance teleport 20ft to backstab any opponent they can physically see. Once they've arrived at their target, normal backstabbing rules apply.

Bat: UMA Special Ability - "And You Get Some Luck Points, And You Get Some Luck Points!: Bat can siphon Luck Points from any vehicle she is physically on and send the Luck Points through the air to any vehicle she can see.

Roll 1d10 for Luck Point Drain: 1 = **2** / 2,3 = **4** / 4,5,6 = **6** / 7,8,9 = **8** / 10 = **10**

Owl: UMA Special Ability - Wargames: Owl may telekinetically take control of any automated construct or vehicle she can physically see but only one vehicle at a time. She may do so by forgoing her attack to make a **Brains Check** to overtake the vehicle's controls and do one of three things.

4) **Brains Check +1** - Kill the engine on any sized vehicle or construct for one turn.

5) **Brains Check +2** - Steer any sized vehicle or control any constructs for one turn.

6) **Brains Check +3** - Control the steering and weapons system of any sized vehicle or any sized construct for one turn.

Hare: UMA Special Ability - My Lovely Assistant: Once per scene, Hare can resurrect a fallen friend, bringing them back to life with **1 Luck Point** and **1 Guts Penalty** by saying a magic word or uttering a phrase. The player should resurrect out of harm's way. That word or phrase is up to the player to decide. Hare may only perform this fantastical trick once per player and no repeat performances.

Once all the players have received their UMA injection read the following:

A shotgun goes off down the hall. The reinforced door buckles under the blast. A video monitor shows a bunch of gang members rushing into the building.

"Not these Urchin idiots again. Take care of them while I get the broadcast-ready."

Jimmy hands you a rifle he had stashed underneath the control console.

7 Urchins will attempt to overtake Kansas City Sounds. They are armed with **shotguns** and **handguns**. Each should have 1-5 luck points, except for their leader Joe Disorder, who will not take damage until the next scene.

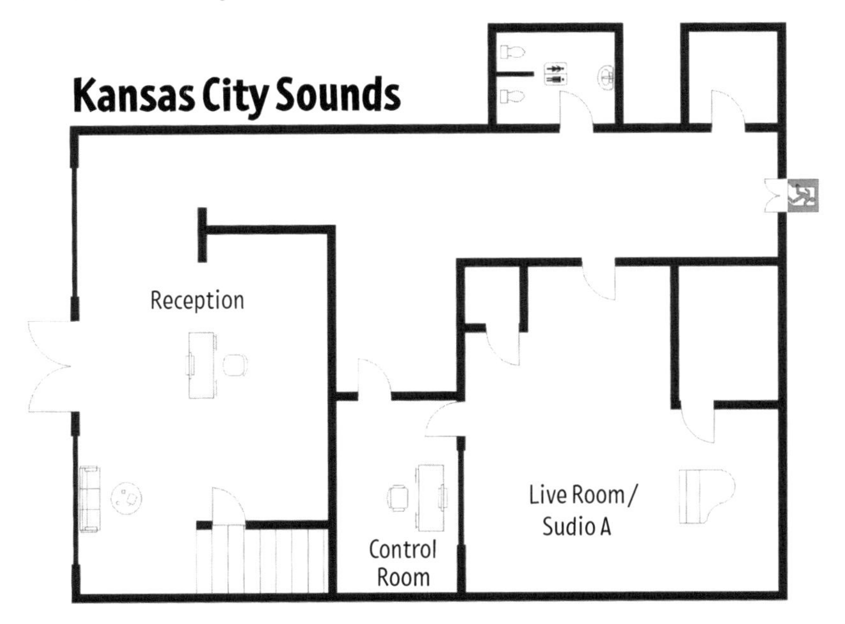

Combat Stage 1: Control Room/Live Room - Studio A: The Urchins split up and attempt to create a kill box between the Control and Live rooms of Studio A. Four Urchins will shoot through the glass from the Live room into the Control room and two Urchins will shoot into the Control Room from the doorframe blocking the exit. Joe Disorder will be shouting orders from the hallway.

Once the Urchins in the Control or Live Room are killed then the others will fall back to the hallway. If only Joe Disorder remains, he will fall back to the Reception Area and 5 more Urchins will show up to reinforce him.

Combat Stage 2: Hallway: This hallway is 60 x 7 with four doors, two on each side, spread one every fifteen feet. The hallway ends at the start of the Reception Area. Two Urchins will be taking cover and shooting from the doorways on each side of the hallway nearest to the Reception Area. Two more will be shooting from both sides of the doorway of the Reception Area itself. The final Urchin will run headlong down the hallway with a handgun in each hand, screaming obscenities as he unloads both magazines. He is an idiot with 1 LP.

Once the idiot and two of the two Urchins in Studio C and D are killed, Joe Disorder will make a break for the door. The gang's vehicles and the rest of the Urchins will be waiting outside.

Combat Stage 3: Reception Area: Whatever Urchin remains will turn their backs in confusion at the sight of their leader running away. Any attacks against them will have a +2 bonus to damage.

When only the Urchin's leader is left standing, read the following:

Scene 3: Grandtheft Hellsing

A whitish-yellow oozing spatter is all over the recording console and the walls. It smells horrible and you try not to retch.

"They shot me? Wow, weird, it doesn't hurt too bad." Jimmy leans back in his chair. You hear a loud pop as his exoskeleton cracks and ooze starts to gush out of him.

"Okay, now that hurts," Jimmy wheezes. "Alright, I think I'm done, which is great because, to be honest, living sixty years as a human/roach hybrid wasn't too fun. Oh wow, okay, that's something I never felt before. That's bad. Focus Jimmy. The one thing I want you to remember was what I was always trying to get across to Croc. You don't need a leader or someone telling you what to do. You are a pack of wild animals! It's time to take back the earth!"

You hear the distinct sound of your rides revving up outside. The Urchins are stealing your rides!

Jimmy shouts for you to get going and then presses a button. There's a clunk as a cassette tape engages and the studio broadcasts the final Hellsings song.

Outside, a kid with a grin that is more empty gums than teeth leans out the driver's side window and yells, "Hey, Hellsings, ya beat!"

This is Joe Disorder.

When the players leave the studio, the rest of the Urchins will have stolen the player's vehicles and left their crappy motorcycles behind. If the players want their vehicles back they will have to give chase (use **Dirtbike** stats). If the players decide not to pursue the Urchins, they lose access to whichever specialty vehicles were stolen from their vehicle array.

If they decide not to pursue their stolen vehicles, read the following:

> You see your vehicles ride off into the sunset without you but you have bigger fish to fry. You've got a technocracy to burn.

GR Notes: The following are optional rules for a more high speed chase in a city encounter. You can have a normal chase encounter where the Hellsings get back their vehicles, but this might make the encounter more claustrophobic. A d10 is rolled at the beginning of the player's turn, and then one of these rules is in effect for that turn. On the next player's turn, you roll again.

Combat Stage 1: Use the Downtown Kansas City Map and the High-Speed Chase City Rules to determine the twists and turns of the road during combat.

GR Notes: The Urchins' leader, Joe Disorder, will claim whichever vehicle is the most powerful for this encounter and leave the rest to his gang. Unless more mem-

Coleman Way
KANSAS CITY
SOUNDS
ST.REED'S
HOSPITA
COMIC EXPLOSION!
Trainer Boulevard
CONNECTIONS
LOOP
Avenue E
S.S.DILLON'S
TATTOOS
Avenue F
Avenue G
BUDDY'S COFFEE
RUTY'S
Avenue H
Reynolds Parkway
Avenue I
ST.MARKS
KANSAS
City!
CITY
GARDENS

bers are added from the High-Speed Chase city rules, there will be one Urchin for each vehicle.

High-Speed Chase - City Rules: At the start of each turn, players must each roll a d10 to determine if they encounter any road hazards while in pursuit.

1-5: Nothing happens

6: Crash into a newsstand or food cart +1 to your **Action Checks** plus 1 **Guts Penalty**

7: Knock an opponent into a wall +1 their **Action Checks** plus 1 **Guts Penalty**

8: Smokescreen fills the street and adds -3 to damage

9: Unfinished Roadwork. All players must make a successful **Action Check** or take **2 Guts Penalties**

10: Another Urchin on a bike enters the battle and tries to commandeer your vehicle

The broadcast starts with a drum beat.

Jimmy's voice comes through your helmets. He's got some reverb and EQ going that makes his voice sound like God.

"They call this place the wasteland but who calls it that? Who named it that? Not us. People who live very far away from us named it that. And do you know why they live far away? 'Cause they ran away. They ran to ivory towers and left us to wallow in empty fields and buildings."

Joe Disorder sticks his head out of the driver's side window, "You hear this garbage, you jerks? I should turn around and blow up that station." He lobs a grenade out his window in a fit of pique.

Once the players commandeer one of their vehicles, read the following:

"We have a different name for the wasteland. We call it home. Right now we got someone living in our home and trying to tell us how to live. How to interact. They turn off the tap to keep us hungry, to keep us fighting, and it worked. Until now! It's time our bands played the same tune. The Black Swans think they run the wasteland, but they don't, and they can't because it is not the wasteland anymore. It's home! It's time to defend our home. Rise and raid The Black Swans. They can't stop all of us. Let's take what's ours. Can you dig it?"

Combat Stage 2: Joe Disorder will try and outrace the Hellsings in whatever vehicle he is currently driving.

"Hey Hellsings, these rides were wasted on you ancient d-bags with your grandpa music." Joe Disorder shouts. He wouldn't know good music if it kicked him in the ass. Fortunately, you are here to teach him a little respect.

Bossfight Joe Disorder

GR Notes: For Joe Disorder's stats, see page 42

Once Joe Disorder is out of Luck Points, read the following:

> Joe Disorder throws a flashbang that has you seeing stars and your ears ringing. When you finally blink away some of the haze after a few seconds, he's gone. As you regain your hearing, you could swear you hear him calling you a bunch of dicks from somewhere far off.

End Of The Episode Wrap-Up And Awards Ceremony

As you wrap for the night or for a quick break before the next episode, have the players roll 1d10 to replenish Luck Points. They may always re-roll a 1. Remember, there is no maximum for Luck Points. You can also do an **End of the Episode Award Ceremony**, letting the group vote, giving out awards for:

Best Action Sequence: +1 Luck Points

Best Commandeering: +2 Luck Points

Best Joke or One Liner: +3 Luck Points

Best Kill: +4 Luck Points

Catch You Next Time!

Episode 6: Kill the Head and the Body Dies

Fox's voice comes through your helmet.

"It's crazy out here. Crow just got eyes in the sky and everyone is attacking Black Swan bases, and I mean everyone! Whether it's revenge, a power grab, or just fun, the swarm is attacking the Swans."

Fox pauses for a moment, as if they can't even believe what they're going to say next.

"But that's not the craziest thing. Crow saw her. He saw the Black Swan, Mrs. Olivia, leaving the Northern HQ, all six foot two with a shock of white hair. Nobody has seen her in a decade. Everyone thought she was a myth. Crow thought maybe he was seeing things, but then she pulled out her rifle, the Nightrider, and took a shot from two goddamn miles away. It cracked through his battery housing and exploded his glider. The explosions cooked him a little and he only survived the fall cause he had his wingsuit. She's the real deal and she's riding the head of a battalion. This is our only opportunity, let's end this!"

GR Notes: This is the final episode. Feel free to let the players know this is the end of the line. The players can pick any rides available so far in the game. Bear can upgrade them however they want.

Scene 1: Swan Song

The Black Swan battalion gathered at the gates of their northern HQ. It's an impressive caravan of vehicles with Mrs. Olivia watching from the battlements.

The dust on the road parts like the Red Sea and you spot the Hexie Coven, a leather-clad witch band from the mountains riding ripper ATVs, arrive on the scene. They swarm and attack the Black Swans. Everyone must have heard the battle call.

Unfazed, Mrs. Olivia pulls out the Nightrider and sets her sights on the group below. She shoots the Red Wolfe, Hexie Coven's leader who was going about sixty miles per hour, right between the eyes.

Mrs. Olivia pulls out a handset and drawls languidly, unhurried or unfazed by the gangs out for her blood. "You Hellsings just don't get it. This is bigger than any little band. Resolv Corp runs the whole show. We need order!"

This is your target!

Combat Stage 1: Three battle-damaged Elite Motorcycles break off from the Hexies conflict after they notice your approach. They will rush the Hellsings with guns blazing and try and prevent you from accessing Mrs. Olivia at all costs while she is busy picking off the Hexies one by one with her Nightrider.

GR Notes: For Mrs. Olivia's Stats, see pg 45 For the Nightrider's stats, see pg. 51

Combat Stage 2: Mrs. Olivia will remain in the tower and turn her attention to the Hellsings. She will directly attack the pilots of any flying vehicles first, using the Nightrider's Special Ability, and then fire off a regular shot at the vehicle. Should there be no flying vehicles during this combat, Mrs. Olivia will always attack the driver of the most significant threat first.

Once Mrs. Olivia is down to half health, read the following:

Mrs. Olivia slips and begins to fall off the tower before catching herself. She quickly regains her composure and prepares to fire another shot from the Nightrider.

"Enough!"

The final Hellsings broadcast abruptly ends.

Thousand-foot plumes of reddish-blue flames erupt from the earth's crust about a mile apart, turning the Black Swans base into a hellscape.

A giant hologram face appears in the sky.

"This is Elliot Tanzeer, CEO of Resolv Corp, speaking. Mrs. Olivia just showed how futile it is to corral rats so we are going ahead with our planned Amortization and Depreciation Plan B. We will dispose of Project Wasteland with Resolv Corp tactical Shiva and Single fire nukes and expense it on our taxes. We'll move forward with the new wasteland project in the Pacific Northwest."

Mrs. Olivia shouts, "You bastard, you said we'd keep everyone alive!" She aims the Nightrider towards the Black Swans HQ and fires.

A spiderweb of glass appears before the hologram's face. "Spectacular! Mrs. Olivia, you were worth every penny. Unfortunately, you must now be terminated." A tower from the base activates and fires a blast at Mrs. Olivia. She falls dead, dropping the Nightrider.

"And for the rest of you, we will not be seeing you next quarter." The ground shakes, and the Black Swans HQ begins to rise into the air.

As the base ascends into the air, the road through its gates begins to stretch and tear, leaving just enough blacktop attached to make a jump. All ground vehicles attempting to enter the base as it rises must make a successful **Action Check +3** or plummet to their death.

Scene 2: Turbo Killer

A few Hexie Coven successfully jump to join you in entering the city as it rises. The rest fall helplessly to their doom into the crater left by the flying base.

All the buildings in the Black Swan base are curved and bent, which makes the Tanzeer tower, a steel and glass monolith emblazoned with the Resolv Corp emblem standing at its epicenter, all the more surreal. It's as if you are looking at it through a warped lens or some ancient looking glass. Either way, it feels claustrophobic and disorienting.

An energy blast hits the road before you, leaving behind a giant crater. When you look to see where it came from, automated sentry towers are coming to life on top of the buildings.

You see a pack of Elite guards riding hoverbikes equipped with deadly-looking Gatling guns charging down the sides of the buildings.

The Hexi Coven engage their rippers.

GR Notes: Because of the buildings' angles, let the players know everything can become a jump if they want to try cinematic attacks or to commandeer.

Tanzeer Elite Guard Hoverbike
7ft Length, 2ft Width, 2ft Height, 480lbs., One Rider

25 LP
Action 8
Brains
Brawn 4
Cool
Charm
Guts 6

Description:The Tanzeer "Elite" Cruiser Motorcycle was initially released in the same wave of vehicles as the Ladybug to compete with Bishop Motorsport's "Brando" Cruiser. It was a colossal failure due to the front wheel cover making it nearly impossible to steer, resulting in the death of four riders, a recall, and a massive settlement payout. Rex Tanzeer, not one to take failure lightly, refused to believe it was the fault of his design. He blamed some of his front-line workers in an unhinged social media post and buried the Elite Bike at the behest of his legal team. Six years later, Tanzeer finally got the handling right after making a breakthrough in hover technology. It has since been repurposed for use by his Elite Guard.

1 Attack or 1 SA Per Turn

Kick/Punch: MV 5ft DMG -6

Gatling Gun: 100 Round Cartridge, DMG -4 The rider will gently squeeze the trigger of the Gatling releasing a controlled burst at their foes.

Special Ability - Cold Steel Rain: Every other turn the rider will fully squeeze the Gatling gun trigger, unleashing a hail of bullets dealing 3 LP damage to all foes unless they can make a successful **Action Check +2** to dodge.

GR Notes: The Gatling gun is more of a cinematic weapon, so while it is said to have a 100-round cartridge, it is at your discretion whether you want to make the player count their bullets.

GR Notes: Hover Vehicles are not limited to using the road and may fly up both flat and curved walls and over obstacles and road hazards easily.

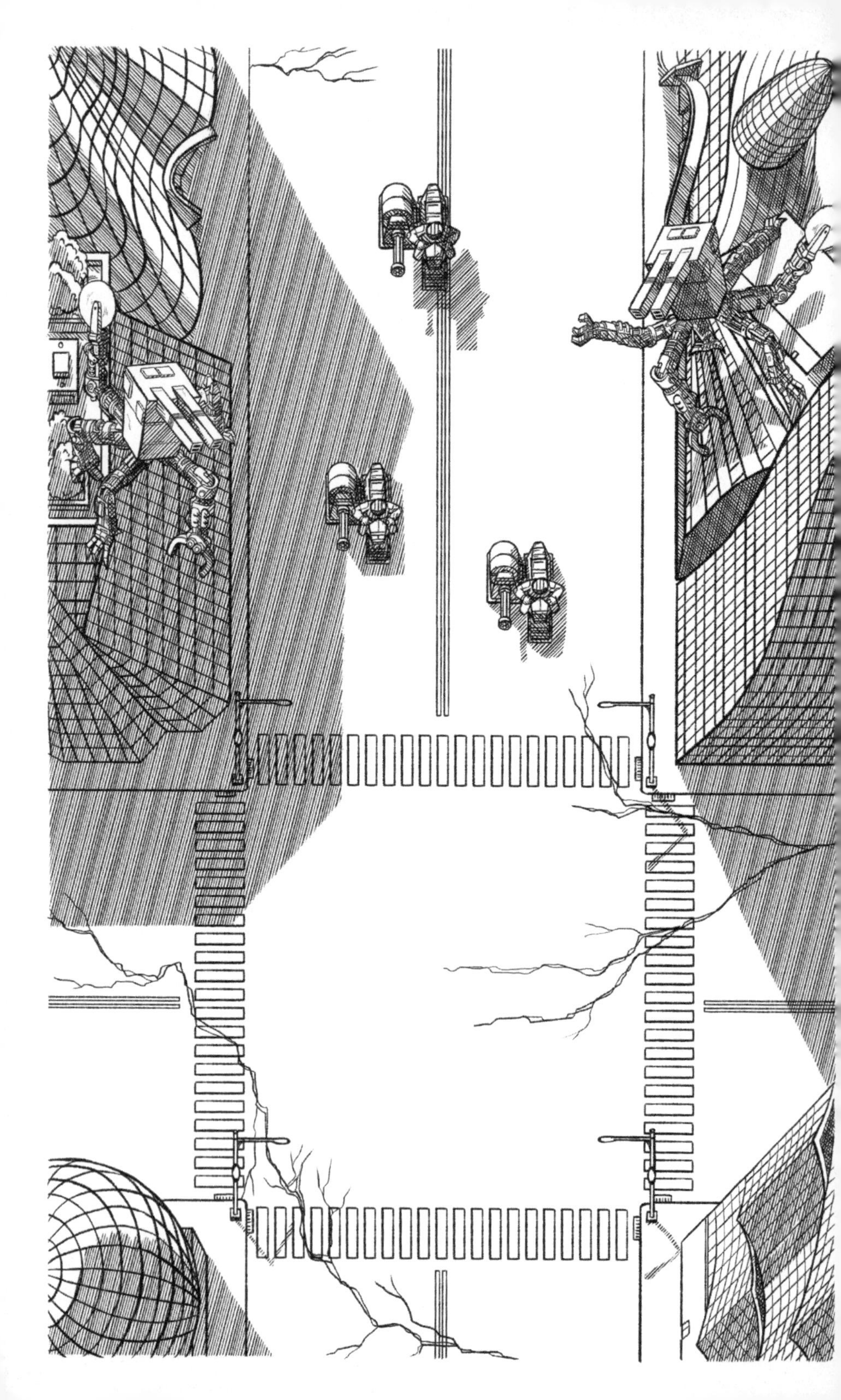

Tanzeer M.O.G.O. (Mobile Offensive Guard Obelisk)

15ft Length, 15ft Width, 15ft Height, 20,000 lbs.

Description: Becoming increasingly paranoid and distrustful of his human bodyguards, Elliot decided he needed something a little more "reliable" for the security of his compound. After staying up for three days straight at his drafting table, he decided to storm the R&D lab with the fruits of his over caffeinated labor. After they stayed up for three more days, fearful of Elliot's manic whimsy, they delivered the initial prototype for a Mobile Offensive Guard Tower. Elliot loved the design but hated the name, so he fired the entire team and rechristened it the M.O.G.O (patent pending).

Action 5

Brains

Brawn 9

Cool

Charm

Guts 9

2 Attack or 1 SA Per Turn

"Pew Pew": DMG -2 M.O.G.O has twin laser cannons mounted to its top and will fire one after the other for a one-two pulsing punch.

Lock Up: When close to an enemy vehicle M.O.G.O. will use its hands to grab onto that vehicle and restrain it, allowing it to do double damage on its next turn. This will also make the grabbed vehicle susceptible to additional +2 damage from other enemy attacks. To break free from the M.O.G.O.'s grip, the player must make a successful **Brawn Check +3**.

Nails On The Chalkboard: DMG -7 M.O.G.O will use its claws to scratch up a vehicle's surface to compromise its structural integrity. Players must make a successful **Guts Check** or suffer 1 **Guts Penalty**.

Pinch Your Cheeks: DMG -6 M.O.G.O. will use its pincher to grab at an enemy vehicle. In addition to damage, the player must successfully make a **Guts Check +1** or suffer 1 **Guts Penalty**.

"The Slice Is Right, Bro": DMG -5 M.O.G.O. will use its buzzsaw attachment to slice up the front end of an enemy vehicle, resulting in damage and an **Action Check +1** to navigate the vehicle out of M.O.G.O.'s carving radius. Failure will result in an +1 penalty to the player's next **Action Check**.

"Torn In Two, And Three, And Four": DMG -4 M.O.G.O. will use its saw attachment to carve up an enemy vehicle. In addition to damage, the saw will dig itself to the vehicle at the end of its tear resulting in a **Brawn Check +1** to break free or the player will take a +2 penalty to their next **Action Check**.

Special Ability - "No Anesthesia": Once per episode, M.O.G.O may make four attacks against a single vehicle in unison. The attack may consist of any combination of attacks that may not exceed four, each at DMG -5. In addition to damage, the player must make a **Guts Check +3** or suffer 2 **Guts Penalties**.

Combat Stage 1: Two automated towers will make a concentrated attack on the flying vehicles first, prioritizing them over those on the ground. If there are no flying vehicles, they will immediately open fire on the ground to slow them down just enough for the three Elite Guard Hoverbikes to catch up and attack. The road will remain flat during this stage.

Once the hoverbikes have been taken out read the following:

As the rising base pierces through some low-lying stratus clouds, everything starts to feel off-kilter. The earth beneath your feet feels as settled as a giant ship can feel while and the earth below that feels like a distant memory.

You see a squad of Hover Cars coming directly at you from the direction of Resolv Tower. They are the last thing standing between you and freedom.

Tanzeer Elite Guard Hover Car

13ft Length, 6ft Width, 4ft Height, 2,500 lbs., Two Riders

30 LP
Action 5
Brains
Brawn 6
Cool
Charm
Guts 7

Description: Once Rex Tanzeer perfected the hover technology, he adapted it to make the world's first flying car; the Tanzeer Black Phoenix. The Phoenix was meant to mark Tanzeer's return to the automotive industry after years of failure with the Elite Cruiser and was set to premiere at the 2048 World's Fair in Chicago, Illinois. This was not meant to be, however, as the event was scrapped due to the escalation of the Amphikura War. Dejected and rejected once again, Tanzeer opted to divest himself from the automotive business. The Black Phoenix has since been weaponized and repurposed for use by Tanzeer's Elite Guard.

1 Attack

Gatling Gun: 100 Round Cartridge, DMG -2 The rider will gently squeeze the trigger of the Gatling releasing a controlled burst at their foes.

SA - Cold Steel Rain: Every other turn, the rider will fully squeeze the Gatling gun trigger, unleashing a hail of bullets dealing 3 LP damage to all foes unless they can make a successful **Action Check +2** to dodge.

GR Notes: The Gatling gun is more of a cinematic weapon, so while it is said to have a 100-round cartridge, it is at your discretion whether you want to make the player count their bullets.

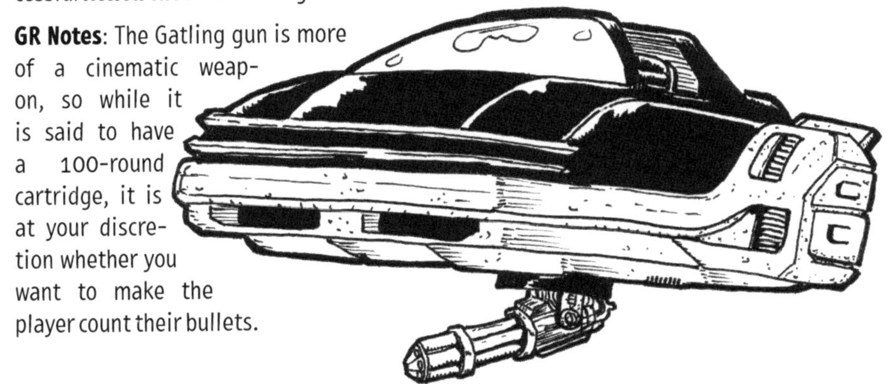

Combat Stage 2: Two Elite Hover Cars enter the fray with a driver and passenger in each car. The driver will use the onboard weapons while the passenger attempts to commandeer the nearest vehicle by using **wing suits** and **grappling guns**.

The base will also shift and bank to the right as it rises, ripping its last bits free from the Kansas soil. Everything anchored to the ground will shift to the left, launching anything unattached in the way of the riders, becoming road hazards. These will affect both flying and ground vehicles. Everyone must make an **Action Check +2** to dodge the debris or take 10 LP damage, 1 **Guts Penalty**, and a +1 Penalty to their next **Action Check**.

Scene 3: Spirit in the Sky

The entire base banks to the west as it ascends to thirty thousand feet. On this tilted axis, you can see all of Kansas below you. Even the Silo, your home, sticks out definitely on the horizon. You imagine Bee in the middle of teaching a class and all the kids staring at the sky, watching this big city ascending to the heavens.

Pitched upwards at a 30-degree angle, the Resolv Corp tower lays in front of you like a smooth staircase. It acts like a long glass runway and your tires dig into the bulletproof reinforced glass. As you race to the top floor, you remember what failure means. Elliot nukes everything. That's not an option.

As if you didn't have enough problems, a twenty-foot armored mech blasts through the glass window of the executive suite right in front of you and you haul the wheel to the right to avoid crashing into it.

"Oh, this is exciting! I get to tech demo the Next Gen Tanzeer Mobile Mech Suit. And I get to get rid of this Hellsing headache while generating some Q4 orders," Elliot says with a laugh. "Now that is multitasking! Please ensure we record this from all angles for the sizzle reel."

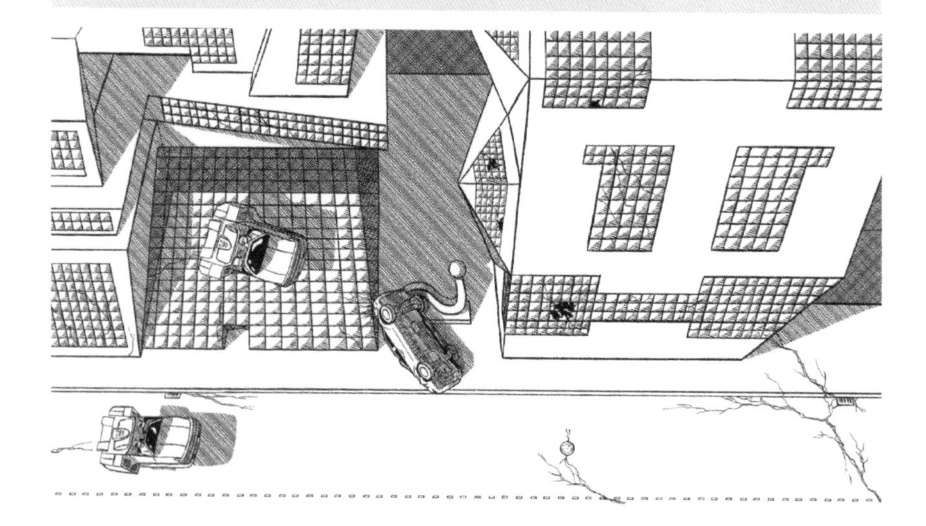

Combat Stage 3: The base makes a hard left bank to the west. All ground vehicles slide towards the nearest buildings and must make an **Action Check +2** to adjust their driving pattern. If they have commandeered a hover vehicle or are in a flying vehicle, it would be an **Action Check +1** to avoid impact and ride sideways up the buildings. If they fail, they crash into the building taking 15 LP Damage, 2 **Guts Penalties**, and a +2 to their next **Action Check**.

As the riders drive up the buildings, two more Automated Guard Towers pop up and open fire on the vehicles as the city begins to bank again.

GR Notes: The city is preparing to make one last trajectory shift and should be held back until the guard towers are defeated.

Combat Stage 4: The city makes a final bank upwards towards the stratosphere in an attempt to pierce it before dropping its nukes on Kansas. This new trajectory will make it nearly impossible for the ground and hover vehicles to keep their traction and will make it difficult for the hover and flying vehicles to adjust.

Flying vehicles must make an **Action Check +2** or crash into the building taking 20 LP damage, 2 **Guts Penalties**, and lose their next turn.

Ground and hover vehicles must make an **Action Check +3** or fall off the city and plummet to their deaths.

Should anybody fail this check, they may dive from their vehicle and can be saved by grabbing onto a Glider or Copter by making an **Action Check +3**.

GR Notes: If no player can save them in this manner, then Crow will be flying by in a Gyrocopter ready to make the save. Crow is only here to rescue and will not attack. With that said, they can surrender their Copter and glide away to safety should a vehicle be needed. The ground will level off after this stage of combat.

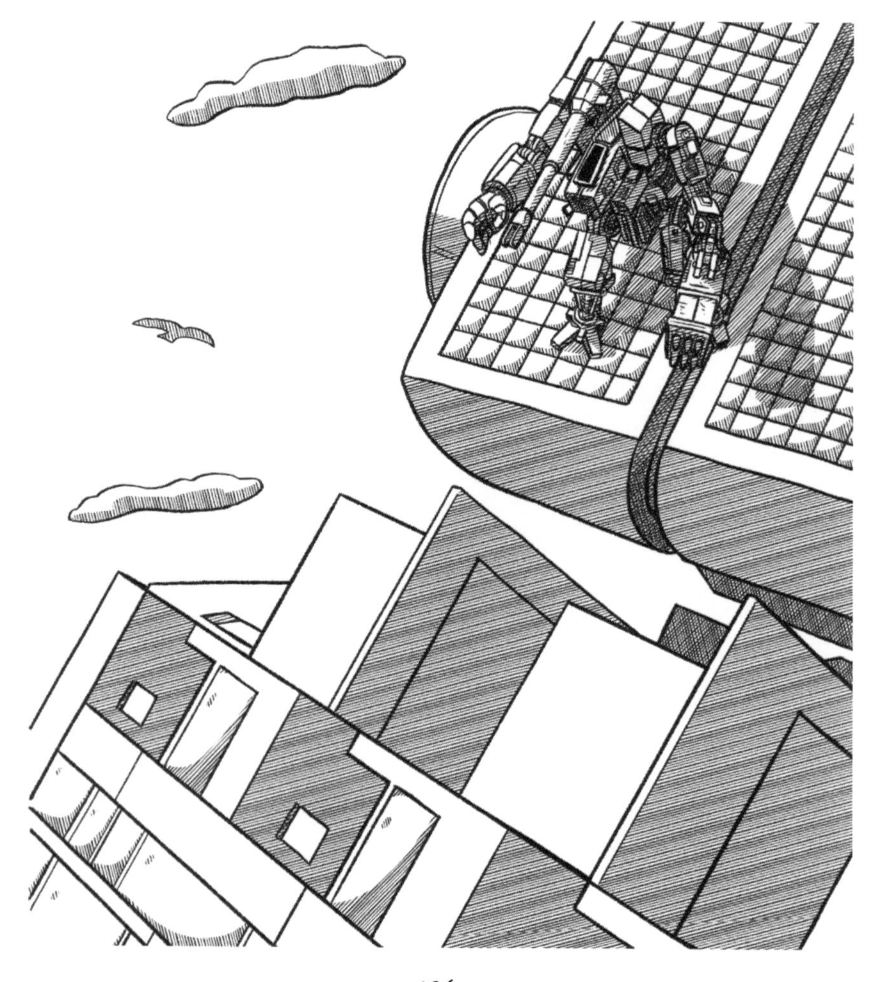

The Colosseum (Mecha Tanzeer)

7ft Length, 15ft Width, 30ft Height, 70,000 lbs., One Rider

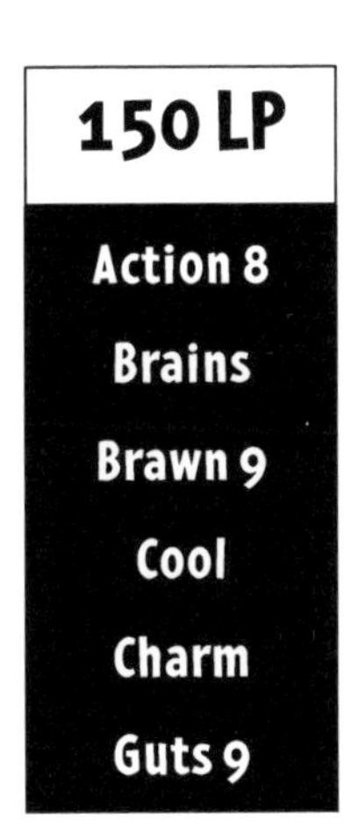

Description: The pinnacle of the Tanzeer family's design prowess came not just from the cars or the architecture or even the new forms of renewable energy; it came from the idea that Elliot could make a real-life version of one of his favorite fighting robots, The Colosseum. The Colosseum was one of seven robots featured in the 2030 animated series, Pacific Knights. The Knights' storyline revolved around human-piloted fighting robots meant to battle kaiju-sized versions of the Amphikura off the Pacific coastline. It was canceled after one season.

2 Attacks and 1 SA Per Turn

Starting Inventory: Missiles

Rock Em' Sock Em' Right Hook: DMG +1 The Colosseum makes a powerful pugilistic punch resulting in damage plus **1 Guts Penalty**.

Kick Kansas: The Colosseum may use its legs to stomp, crush, or punt an enemy vehicle.

> **Crush**: DMG +3 Ground vehicles must make an **Action Check +2** to dodge this attack or suffer 2 **Guts Penalties** in addition to damage.
>
> **Punt**: DMG +5 The Colosseum must make an **Action Check +3** to attempt to punt a ground vehicle. Failure to do so will result in the Colosseum falling over and taking 10 LP damage plus 1 **Guts Penalty**.

If successful, its target must make an **Action Check +3** to dodge this attack or be launched into the air aimed at the nearest flying vehicle. The flying vehicle must make an **Action Check +3** to dodge this attack, or they will take DMG +10 and 3 **Guts Penalties**. If the ground vehicle isn't immediately wasted, or there is no flying vehicle in range, it will crash land, taking an additional 10 LP damage and 1 **Guts Penalty**.

Lightning Laser: DMG +7 The Colosseum may unleash the electric fury of manufactured lightning upon its enemies once every other turn. In addition to damage, players must make a **Guts Check +3** or suffer 1 **Guts Penalty**.

Special Ability - Missile Fist!: 6 Missiles, DMG +9 The Colosseum may launch one missile per turn at full strength or fire off all six at once, each at DMG -4

Once Elliot Tanzeer is down to half his luck points read the following:

Just as taking out the Colosseum seemed impossible, a quartet of missiles slams into its side, leaving a cloud of smoke and fire from the burning metal and plastic. When it clears, you see the missile assault destroyed the top part of the Colosseum suit and exposed part of the cockpit and Elliot's head.

A helicopter gunship hovers nearby. Its rotor blades are engaged in stealth mode and are almost silent.

Scorp says, "You need any help?" over the loudspeaker.

Elliot is visibly angry. He retaliates with scramble missiles which Scorp narrowly dodges.

GR Notes: Once Elliot's head is exposed, he can be attacked directly by the Nightrider.

Elliot Tanzeer

72ft Length, 15ft Width, 14ft Height, 20,000 lbs. 20 LP

20 LP
Action 5
Brains 8
Brawn 4
Cool 4
Charm 6
Guts 4

Description: Elliot is the brilliant CTO of Resolv Corp. He differs from his family in that he cares more about technology and less about the corporate world. That did not mean he wasn't corrupt though. He masterminded the wasteland as a project to test out new equipment and to gain insights into human nature.

Starting Inventory: **Handgun**, Money Clip With $5,000 Cash, Satellite Phone

Special Ability - "Let's Make a Deal": Elliot is so wealthy that he has zero issues with paying to make a problem disappear. Once per episode, he may attempt to buy off any or all assailants by offering whatever their heart desires. There are zero guarantees this will work but you miss 100% of the shots you don't take, amirite?

Once Elliot is down to 0 luck points read the following:

The nuclear powered suit seizes up and freezes around Elliot. Its joints begin to glow a sickly bright green before it loses balance and falls off the Resolv Tower, plummeting towards the earth. Once he is at a good distance, his suit explodes.

With Elliot gone, the base's rocket engines begin to sputter.

"Of course, he tethered the city's flight controls to his suit! What a megalomaniac! Get on!" Scorp maneuvers the chopper to you and opens the cargo bay door.

The city begins to fall and break up as you hurry to get on board. Scorp flies you out of there, dodging raining debris and eventually landing in a deserted field. The city crashes into the earth with a boom that can be heard for miles, releasing a huge plume of smoke into the sky that soon blends into the omnipresent dust bowl cloud haze.

Scorp gets out of the copper and says, "The end of the world tried to come to Kansas, but it looks like you Hellsings bought us all a little extra time. I guess you are the real deal."

Scorp holds out his hand and asks, "It's about time we had a little peace in the midwest. We cool?"

GR Notes: They could accept, deny, or kill Scorp. Whatever the players choose won't change much.

End Of The Episode Wrap-Up And Awards Ceremony

As you wrap for the night or for a quick break before the next episode, have the players roll 1d10 to replenish Luck Points. They may always re-roll a 1. Remember, there is no maximum for Luck Points. You can also do an **End of the Episode Award Ceremony**, letting the group vote, giving out awards for:

Best Action Sequence: +1 Luck Points

Best Commandeering: +2 Luck Points

Best Joke or One Liner: +3 Luck Points

Best Kill: +4 Luck Points

Epilogue 1 Dishes are Done, Man

You wake up in your bunks at the Silo. Everything seems to be going slowly back to normal, or so you thought. Bee comes into your room and says, "Hey, you gotta see this".

You look out of the window and see a mile-long convoy made up of members of different bands.

"We, uh, have some new recruits, All looking to join the Hellsings," Bee says, laughing.

You remember Crocs' vision about a million wild animals roaming the midwest and smile at his memory. Maybe it's just crazy enough to work.

Epilogue 2 And Onto the Next

A month later, Crow comes and tells you he heard word from your Waikiki Chapter. There's some trouble brewing in the ocean. The chapter leader, Shark, has gone missing but Crab and his crew can take care of it.

See you Hellsings next time in **Minisub Mania!**

Epilogue 3 Post Credits

Back in Kansas City Sounds, The Hellsings broadcast suddenly cuts off.

Silence.

The rolling chair holding Jimmy Larouche's body tips backward, precariously teetering off balance until physics wins and it falls to the ground.

There's a loud thud, the sound of a human-sized roach corpse hitting the hardwood.

From the floor, Jimmy Larouche yells "fuck!"

CATCH YOU NEXT TIME!

Top Row L to R: Bee, Wolf, Croc, Bear, Cub, Boar, Crow, & Fox
Bottom Row: Dog, Hare, Bat, Cat, Rat, & Owl

Credits

Written by Geo Collazo & John McGuire

Art by

Ed Bickford

Tim Burns

Sally Cantirino

Claire Connelly

Marie Enger

Charles Ferguson Avery

Teresa Guido

Cheese Hasselberger

Lou Morgue

Dan Smith

Nick Tofani

Wack! Artwork

Character Design by Sally Cantirino

Cover by Sally Cantirino

Vehicle Desing by Tim Burns

Road Maps by Skull Dixon

City & Studio Maps by Hambone

Story Editing by Meghan Ball

Layout by Cheese Hasselberger

Logo Design by Christina Imperiale

Cultural Consultation by James Mendez Hodes

Beta Readers: Clay Fleischer, Shane Welin.

Play Testers: Sally Cantirino, Ian Gonzales, Lou Morgue, Josh Goldfarb, Josh Look, Adam Rose, Meghan Ball, Carrie Howell.

Special thanks to Jennifer Sisco, Sally Cantirino, Levi Combs, Tony Vasinda, Shane Welin, Matt Kelley, Banana Chan, Adam Vass, and you for Kickstarting this game.

Thank You

Derek Kinsman, Ian Gonzales, Banana Chan, Kenneth Means, Jay Domingo, Ben Cartwright, Brian Elmore, Jim Fortsas, Crazy Matt Reed, Clay Fleischer, Levi Combs, Christopher M, Wolf Manzella, Sean McG, Chieana, Jeff Baker, Josh Look, Chuck Kranz, PANTS, Henry Strong, Josh F, Otto Hasselberger, Tyler Vance, George Koroneos, Joe Kontor, Schubacca, Charlie, Shane Welin, Joshua Eschen, Grim & Perilous Studios, Michael Isaacs, Mark Kinney, Nerdstorm!, M Bielaczyc, Mönster Sküll, Andrew M. Reichart, Paul R. Smith, Dean Browell, Mark Sable, Christopher Bloise, Brian Colin, Martin Prucha, Thomas Paul, Adam Vass, Low Pickett, Noble Knight Games, Jojo Gwiazdowski, P-Schizzle, Dominic Lopez, Jake Metterville, Jacob Holloway, Alexa Benzaid-Williams, Alberto De Jesus, Paige Connelly, Dustin Colwell, CCB, Phillip McGregor, Steve Albertson the Dragon Warrior of Epic Levels, Tom Sowonja, Andrew Diaz, J. Colquhoun, Beastie Moto, Eric Swanson, Bob Kidd, Jason Brauncowski, ViscountEric, Jason Doucette, OldCrow, Bryan Marshall, PIDayScott, Stephen Morse, ELF Vesala, Alex Wilson, Chris Beaman, Olympic Cards and Comics, Doc Wigard, Jacob Marks, Jarek Ejsymont, Max Traver, Brian Shutter, Jeremy "Father Goose" Shuman Jr., Third Kingdom Games, Elijah Dixon, Xavier R, Jeremy Van Buskirk, Larry Haught, Pete Jones.

3,2,1... ACTION!

CHARACTER NAME:

PLAYER NAME:

1 2 3

HOW GUTS WORKS

1-2 - You're OK!
3 - Ouch! -1 to your stats.
4 - You DIE!

ACTION BRAINS COOL

BRAWN CHARM GUTS

ROLL = OR BELOW YOUR STAT

HEADSHOT:

USE LUCK POINTS HERE

Push your luck, but don't let it run out!

SPECIAL ABILITY:

INVENTORY:

WEAPONS:	DMG:	SPECIAL ATTACK:
1.		
2.		
3.		
4.		

A BACKSTORY IN THREE SENTENCES:

1.

2.

3.

NOTES & DOODLES: